It was Dad.

He was still wearing the Armani slacks from Monday, pleated front. With them, his faded Hickory Fork Consolidated athletic department sweatshirt, and his old, beat-up gym shoes, Keds. He had a little pile of stones beside him, and he was pitching them into the brown water. Every once in a while, *plop*, and the creek swallowed another stone. Dad's face was as gray as the day. I almost didn't know him because he's always looked ahead, but not now.

We stood out of sight. Even Brick didn't run on to throw his arms around Dad's neck. The three of us stood there until the pile of stones next to Dad began to run out.

Then we backed off and headed home the other way around. Now we knew, even Bambi. We wouldn't be leaving Hickory Fork anytime soon.

Bambi stalked on ahead. It reminded me of when she walks on the set, and maybe she doesn't know her lines, but she's willing to wing it.

Brick was keeping up, at least with me. Just as we'd found Bates Gulch Road again, he motioned for me to bend down. "I hate that school, Buffie," he whispered. "Those people eat their own."

| | | | |
|---|---|---|---|
| | | | |
| | | | |
| | | | |
| | | | |
| | | | |
| | | | |
| | | | |
| | | | |
| | | | |
| | | | |
| | | | |
| | | | |
| | | | |

# BEL-AIR BAMBI
# AND
# THE MALL RATS

## Richard Peck

Published by
Bantam Doubleday Dell Books for Young Readers
a division of
Bantam Doubleday Dell Publishing Group, Inc.
1540 Broadway
New York, New York 10036

The trademark Laurel-Leaf Library® is registered in the U.S. Patent and Trademark Office.

The trademark Dell® is registered in the U.S. Patent and Trademark Office.

ISBN: 0-440-21925-6

RL: 5.7

Reprinted by arrangement with Delacorte Press

Printed in the United States of America

April 1995

10  9  8  7  6  5  4  3  2  1

OPM

*for Jo Ellen and Steve Ham*

# Chapter
# One

**P**icture the scene.

Hands—claws, maybe—draw the curtain back.

A figure forms in the ghastly ruins of the room. Only a black shape and then an outline and then, perhaps, a woman. She wears a long black preworn shroud, cut low in front and lightly singed at the tattered hem. In life she'd been beautiful. Her black hair, though long buried, has a few highlights.

As she raises her arms halfway to heaven, her batwing sleeves fall back to reveal the charred stumps where her hands had been. She must be somebody's mother because she's staring dead-eyed into the distance for her lost children. There seems to have been a fire because the room still smolders. Her complexion is ashen, with actual ashes. Now she's pointing one of her stumps straight at you.

The light around this ghastly mother begins to fade, but now another figure forms at her side. A man—or something that used to be a man. His blackened clothes are grave stained, and his whole head makes Freddy Krueger look like Tom Cruise.

Dimly, at the far end of the room, cobwebby French doors look out on a garden planted in tombstones, all gray with hanging moss. A path meanders up from a swamp. Figures are crawling along this path, heading this way. Three figures: one small, one medium, one a little chunky.

The doors fall open, and these three enter the room. They are the dead children of the corpse parents. The small one is in the lead. There's nothing human about him at first, only an irregular blob. Then he becomes somewhat child-like. A five-year-old, maybe a small six.

He's green and greener still around the lips. He scuttles, humpbacked, into the room, pulling himself along on one elbow and two knees, leaving a trail of dark slime behind. This little wet gnome-shape rests for a moment on an elbow and then looks up, training three sad eyes on his parents. He opens green lips to speak. But only about a pint of swamp water gurgles out instead.

The next child lurching behind him is, if anything, worse. She may be the sister of the little green three-eyed gnome. At one time she wasn't bad-looking, but she's been in a truly terrible accident. Her blood-soaked prom dress is off-white with a pink sash, and she's dragging a leg, hers. You don't dare give her more than a glimpse, but there's worse to come.

Apparently these two have another sister. This is the chunky one. All her arms and legs are tangled in spiderwebs, which slow her down some. Her head, blue, is swollen to gigantic size, stretching all her wretched features tight. She's spidery to a fault. Her legs are black and hairy, and there are far too many of them.

Now the awful parents are turning to their dreadful children. Wind wells up from the swamp, whining. Or maybe it's organ music. The charred mother's black lips part as she starts to greet her children. But then another voice cuts across hers.

"Cut!" Marla, the script girl, barks, walking onto the set. "Kill the lights. Pull the plug on that smoke machine."

On the set the five of us all hold our poses a moment longer. The cameras swing away from us, and the hot lights overhead die out. The last wisp of artificial smoke trails away into the studio rafters. We won't be filming any more today, maybe ever.

Up till then we were the actors in my dad's television production company. Mom and Dad were playing the mom and dad in the script, and we children were the children.

Now Marla was handing Dad two memos. He was still half in character with his Freddy Krueger head in place.

One of the memos was Marla's resignation. The other was from the sheriff of Los Angeles County.

I guess we should have seen this coming. The recession, for one thing. For another, Dad was way over budget, and the word was out. Nobody in the Business wanted to do lunch with him anymore, or take a meeting. The only people Dad saw now were big guys in short socks and pin-striped suits with shoulder holsters. And they weren't from Bank of America.

But Dad had thought he had one more pilot in him. A pilot's a show you get in the can to take to the bank. You film one to show to a network or a cable company. Then you hope they'll pick it up and rain some production money on you. Then you can do a whole series.

The word around Hollywood was always that Dad did his best work on family-togetherness type material. But I have to say, this last pilot we were shooting wasn't Dad's best work. He couldn't hire talent anymore because he couldn't pay union scale. That's why the five of us were the cast, with a single set and preworn costumes. Frankly, Dad was getting desperate. That's why he had gone with the concept of combining family togetherness with Stephen King. The pilot we were doing was basically *The Simpsons* with dead people, if you can follow that.

Except for my little brother, Brick, we're all in the top percentiles verbally. So we were all pitching in to write the script as we went along. Dad couldn't afford writers anymore either.

Dad produced and Mom directed, which is pretty much like any family. I'm not really an actress. What I am is a sixth-grader. I'm sort of a tall-child type. In fact, I am a tall child.

It's my sister, Bambi, who thinks she's the next Jodie Foster. And, boy, is she verbal. She was a little starlet before I was born. At the age of one she was the First Bite baby-food spokesbaby. Her picture was on the label of every jar of First Bite baby food. You couldn't pick up four ounces of mashed banana without seeing Bambi's baby face. Frankly, I don't think she ever got over it. She's still so into camera angles that she can hardly look you in the eye.

But I don't think I'm much of an actress. I like pretending, though, and it's fun being somebody else—even a dead girl in a prom dress. At least she was in high school. But they just wrote me into the script when they couldn't hire talent. Mom and Dad don't want us to be spoiled Hollywood brats, though it may be too late for Bambi. They'd really like us just to be kids, if we could afford it.

Up till that afternoon when the sheriff shut us down, we'd been your basic California family. After high school Dad had hitchhiked west to attend the UCLA film school on a football scholarship. Mom came out as the runner-up in the Miss New Jersey Cranberry pageant. Her prize was a screen test, and she stayed on, going to auditions.

They met on the set of a daytime soap, *San Fernando Valley Where Dreams Die*, which was a downmarket *Santa Barbara*. They were just a couple of kids at the time. Dad was a young gofer with hope in his heart. Mom was understudying a walk-on part.

They got married, and Dad started his climb to the top. Pretty soon he was producing prime-time, and people were offering him percentages of gross. Mom was doing some on-camera work between babies. There are three of us: Bambi, Buffie, and Brick, which aren't unreasonable names if you were born in L.A.

You probably know Dad best as the creator of *Little House in the 'Hood*. It's the one about this family of urban pioneers gentrifying a three-bedroom inner-city colonial. We only got thirteen weeks out of it, but you can still catch it on cable.

Dad also did *Orbit to the End of Time*, that fact-based miniseries on the Russian cosmonauts who got left up in space when the Soviet Union fell apart. *TV Guide* said he reached new heights with it.

Dad did about as much quality work as television allows. Valerie Bertinelli usually had a script she wanted him to look at. But he was always a lot more creative than cost-conscious. As he says, the Business is all peaks and valleys. Now, though, we seemed to be in Death Valley.

On the afternoon they turned off the lights on the set for the last time, the magic seemed to go out of everything. Filming a pilot is hard work. Right away, though, I missed it. The few crew still left cut out early to get to the unemployment office before it closed. It was just the five of us on our own: Dad, Mom, Bambi, Buffie, and Brick, with our pilot totaled. So we moved closer together. We were all still in costume and full makeup, which was weird, though now we were just dark shadows.

Dad's arm was around Mom, and they were both reaching out for us. Brick drew near Mom's knee. Then Mom and Dad began to sing their own personal signature tune, "Do You Know the Way to San Jose?" Things looked bad, but they were worse than that.

The studio was rented space, and we all had to use the same dressing room. I helped Brick get out of his makeup and costume. He had a little beige suede humpback and that extra eyeball stuck down on his cheek with spirit gum. Though he can't get out of his hump by himself, he could peel off his own eye. But he likes the attention. He's six.

I was still easing the scar off my face when Bambi was out of her spider legs and back in her school uniform. Just how serious this situation was hadn't hit her yet. Things hit her hard, but rarely on the first take. She was hogging the

7

mirror, combing her hair up with Vita Care Super Spritz and topping it off with a plastic barrette. She's in eighth grade, so, I mean, image is everything.

We both went to the Stars of Tomorrow School for Girls in the Performing Arts. Bambi insisted on going there because she definitely sees herself as a star of tomorrow. Mom said I should go there, too, so we'd be on the same schedule and have the same commute. And I'd said, "Right, Mom, I'll try to keep an eye on her."

So Bambi and I wore the same school uniform, though it didn't look the same on me. Bambi says I have no fashion sense. And if I don't have it by sixth grade, forget it. Our jackets were Chanel, and her skirt was thigh-high, with panty hose. This being L.A., we'd both been wearing panty hose and blusher since second grade. In panty hose and blusher I look like two wrinkled toothpicks on fire, but I had to try. Just going to the same school with me was hard enough on Bambi.

Brick went to Sandpile Alternative Academy. Mom thought that in a lite-pressure setting, he might gift-out. He's a quiet kid. Even in the pilot he had a nonspeaking part. His hump and the extra eye established his character.

In our sitcom Mom wasn't playing pretty, but she is pretty, though don't mention this around Bambi. Mom was out of her shroud and reaching for her Ray Bans when Dad said, "Take everything," since we couldn't afford to store it.

He backed up the company van to the loading dock, and we loaded up our tacky costumes, the props, cue cards, wigs, smoke machine. Mom swept all our makeup into a grocery bag from Farmers' Market. We picked the place clean. It was like a sale at Ralph Lauren. Bambi wouldn't help. She was already in the van. There were only four seats, and she wanted one.

We headed home ahead of the rush hour. As we drove in through the gates of Bel-Air, things seemed usual. Up on our street, Moraga Drive, though, things weren't usual at all.

Dad braked the van at the foot of our long, curving drive. It was a really nice hilltop property: Early Hollywood French Provincial with separate Jacuzzis for everybody. And a screening room. You could have driven the van into Bambi's walk-in closet upstairs. Heated pool.

Bambi and I were in the backseat but not fighting. Brick's small for six, so he was up front on Mom's lap. Looking up the hill to our house she said, "I don't think the children should see this." So we all looked. The notice on the lawn was signed by the sheriff of L.A. County. Dad geared down. The front door of the house was padlocked, and there was another sign you could read from here:

**ATTEMPTED ENTRANCE UPON THESE
PREMISES IS A CRIMINAL OFFENSE**

We crept around to the garage. All the doors were open, and it was empty inside.

Dad's Jag was missing. He gave a little shrug, and his shoulders looked really tired. Mom's Lexus LS 400 was gone too. So was the customized '57 Chevy, the MG, the lawn tractor, Brick's British bike with the training wheels—all out of there.

We pulled up behind the house. They'd left the pool, but that was about all. There were official seals on all the sliders and the back door. We climbed out of the van, staggering a little. Then it dawned on Bambi. "I've got to get inside."

"Honey," Mom said.

"We've got to sleep somewhere, don't we?"

"They'll have taken the beds," Mom said. In a quick glance she'd noticed the window treatments were gone from the windows.

"Okay," Bambi said, willing to be reasonable. "But I have to get some clothes. Just ten or fifteen changes and all my shoes."

"They'll be gone too."

"Wait a minute." Bambi's hand clutched her forehead. "What about my framed posters—Faith No More, L. L. Cool . . . JON BON JOVI WITH HIS SHIRT OFF?"

"No more," Mom echoed.

That's when Bambi keeled over backward on the crushed marble barbecue environment and started kicking the air.

I thought about Boris and Dolores, too, our husband-and-wife housekeepers. Their Sundance was gone, and so were they. I guessed they'd made a clean break. They always wanted to be paid in cash.

Dad came back from the garage, shaking up a spray can of black touch-up. He hunkered down by the van door to spray out the name of our production company. He was covering up the evidence that this '87 van with a tailpipe in trouble was the only major appliance we had left.

Somehow we were all back in the van, even Bambi. Her face was wet, but her sobs were dry. Mom was going through her own purse—Gucci, not that it mattered now. "I have about eighty dollars and a traveler's check," she said. "We have."

I had a twenty pinned to my underwear, which I always did in case I had to take a cab. Bambi hadn't been shopping yet today, so she had a wad, though sharing was a hard concept for her. Dad had only chicken feed because he always signed for everything. Brick peered around at each of us, possibly adding it up in his mind. He was counting something on his fingers.

"Anyway, at least we have a roof over our heads," I said, meaning the van. Bambi jabbed me, hard. Dad released the emergency so we could coast down the driveway before we had to start burning gas. Though where we were going was anybody's guess.

When we swung out onto Moraga, we nearly had a fender-bender with an oncoming Seville. "Oh, boy"—Dad sighed, kicking the van into life—"everybody down on the floor."

So we all looked out to see that the Seville was full of big guys in pinstripes and bulging shoulders. Now their car was trying to make a U-turn in Moraga Drive.

Dad laid rubber all the way down Stone Canyon Road to the Bel-Air Hotel. I didn't know the van had that kind of acceleration. When we shot out onto Sunset, it's a good thing there was no cross traffic. Now we were running for our lives, but I still didn't know where.

Dad was switching lanes like a teenager. Mom had Brick in a head hold. "Were those guys—"

"Big-time bill collectors," Dad said. "Extra-heavy muscle. I owe some of the guys over in Vegas." We roared past the Beverly Hills Hotel, trying to get ahead of as many cars as possible.

By evening we were out of the smog, on Route 15 heading for 40. When we finally decided we weren't going to be blown away by big-time bill collectors, we got quiet. Bambi dozed. At Victorville we stopped at a Rib Ranch for some takeout. We were driving in the dark by then, and Bambi was dozing again.

"It's happening a lot these days," Mom said quietly. "All over the country. One day you're working. The next day you're not. And besides, show business doesn't make anybody any promises."

Dad's shoulders looked tireder than ever. "Still," he said, "I overextended. I got carried away. I thought it couldn't happen to us."

That brought Bambi around. Either that or she was talking in her sleep. "It couldn't happen to Amber Armitage. If the sheriff of L.A. County impounded her shoes, she'd get her lawyer on the case. Amber has her own lawyer, from that time she had to take her parents to court."

Nobody asked Bambi why Amber had had to take her own parents to court, and she dozed again. We have to hear a lot about Amber Armitage, who is Bambi's best friend when they're speaking.

Just getting away from L.A. and the extra-heavy muscle in the Seville had been enough as long as there was daylight. But now it was night. The highway was a long V ahead into the unknown, thundery with trucks.

I wondered where we were heading, but I was scared to ask. In fact, I was just scared. Could we make it all the way to New Jersey, where Mom came from? New Jersey's next to New York. Maybe there'd be work for Dad there—filming documentaries on subway crime, something like that. But I didn't know if we could pay for the gas to get there. At times like this you wonder what you were worrying about yesterday.

Mom's hand was on the back of Dad's neck. Brick was up on her knee, riding shotgun. And Dad was talking again, this time almost to himself. "It wasn't a bad little town when I was growing up. A long way from anywhere else, but we made our own fun."

So he sure wasn't talking about L.A.

"Little League, National Honor Society, Future Farmers of America, pom-pom girls. A movie Saturday night, maybe a sock hop. Fresh air and four seasons. It was middle America, but what did we know? Listen, it was a pretty darn wholesome place for kids."

So then I knew where we were heading. We were going back to Dad's hometown, two thousand miles from L.A., from anyplace. Where else did we have to go?

I tried to picture it. Everybody in gingham aprons and pigtails, drinking well water. I pictured Dorothy and her little dog Toto before all that wind. Somehow none of this seemed too likely.

I pictured picket fences and Grandma Babcock, Dad's mother. We hadn't seen her since we were babies. She didn't fly out to L.A. because of airport terrorists. We were traveling through unknown territory to a place called Hickory Fork. Really. With sock hops. A pretty darn wholesome place for kids growing up. From the corner of my eye I checked on Bambi, in Chanel and a coma.

We bypassed Needles in the darkest part of night before

**14**

we crossed the state line. Brick spoke then, for us all, his soft good-bye to all we knew and the total California experience.

"Happy trails and save the whales."

# Chapter
# Two

*B*ack in L.A. we'd still have had a couple of months of really good beach weather ahead of us. Here in the country around Hickory Fork it seemed to be early autumn, with trees turning red and yellow behind fix-it shops.

Bambi had slept through most of the trip, two nights and a day on the road. Sitting up in full school uniform, she could be out like a light. I couldn't even get comfortable. My panty hose were traveling more than we were.

We seemed to be driving through the outskirts of town. But Hickory Fork turned out to be all outskirts. It may have been morning rush hour too: four uncustomized pickups and a yellow school bus labeled HICKORY FORK CONSOLIDATED SCHOOL DIST.

Brick was interested. He perched on Mom's knee with his nose against the windshield, taking it all in.

"Down the hill by the bridge," Dad said, "is the VFW where we used to have our school dances. The whole community came." The thought of adults allowed in to a school dance shocked Bambi awake. Her eyes flew open. I could see that Dad was trying to talk up Hickory Fork so we'd like it, or at least not hate it, or something.

But when we went past the VFW, it wasn't there. Instead there was a new windowless building with a metal gate over the door and a sign. "What's a Penny-Pincher Val-U-Mart?" Bambi asked.

Mom was looking too. "A store."

Bambi thought. "No. If it was a store, I'd have heard of it."

We were crossing water now. Don't picture anything quaint, like a covered bridge with planks. This was rusted-out metal over a creek. Looking down, Dad said, "I'd remembered it as a river."

"What's its name?" Mom asked, trying to get up for all this.

"Water Moccasin Branch," Dad replied.

Two guys were crossing the bridge on foot, so Bambi looked. They were older, or at least bigger. One of them was bald. Bambi checked for the label on their Levi's, but there wasn't one. I checked to see if they were carrying lunch buckets. This could be a school day, even here. It may even have crossed my mind that we might be going to school here.

It didn't cross Bambi's. Things were happening too fast

for her. If Dad had given her some lead time about moving away and starting a new school, she could have mounted a campaign against it. There was a half block of paving in downtown Hickory Fork, but now we were heading up a road with ditches.

Grandmothers can be great. Like a grandmother who bakes, and lets you drink all the colas you want without ever mentioning diabetes. Jolly ladies who keep their grandchildren's crayon drawings under cute magnets on the refrigerator. Grandmothers who laugh a lot and like Vanna White and cats. This was Mrs. Rosalee Hatfield, and she lived next door to our grandma Babcock.

They both lived up on Bates Gulch Road. In front of Grandma Babcock's house was a torn-down picket fence and a post for a missing mailbox. We pulled up in a dirt yard next to her Plymouth Duster. It was time to get out of the van, though I was missing it already. Mrs. Rosalee Hatfield from next door was on her porch, looking over and waving a tea towel.

"Is that young Bill Babcock, the big Hollywood typhoon?" she said, meaning Dad. She had a big smile all over her big face. "And my land, your wife and all your chilrun."

So you could see that Hickory Fork didn't need a newspaper or a radio station.

"See any changes, honey?" she yelled over to Dad. It looked like some of the houses along Bates Gulch had burned down. "We call it 'Widows' Row' now!" Mrs. Hatfield threw back her head and laughed merrily. "Blanche is going to be as tickled as a pup to see you all."

Blanche, I remembered, was Grandma Babcock's name. Bambi quivered. Mom too.

I haven't mentioned it, but people always do. Mom and Dad both have a lot of star quality and audience appeal. They're great-looking people, unless they're doing character parts. Here on the third day on the road, there wasn't a crease in Mom's blouse. And off-camera she never wears makeup. She has great hair, too, and just enough. Dad always says he married the only natural blonde in L.A. She wears it smooth and loose. She can just run her hand through it, and, pow, she's Christie Brinkley.

We were on the porch now, and the front door was opening. It was Grandma Babcock in a pantsuit and a new permanent. "I knew it was somebody," she remarked. "I heard Rosalee bawlin' like a calf."

In the smallest voice he'd ever used, Dad said, "Hi, Mama."

She scanned us through her trifocals and noticed we didn't have any luggage.

"Don't tell me," she said. "I figured this would happen sooner or later." Brick was too short to notice, but she zeroed in on Bambi and me. Though the seat of my panty hose was down between my knees, we were still in our school uniforms. What else did we have? "How come you dress them two alike? Are they twins? I forget."

Grandma Babcock had a plastic purse in her hand and started through it. "Make yourselves at home," she said. "I'm late for work anyhow. Let's see, have I got everything?" She dug through her purse. "Wallet, folding plastic head-scarf, hair spray, tire patch, Tylenol, Mace, keys, York peppermint patty, Kleenex, Preparation—"

Mace?

Grandma Babcock worked at the Hickory Fork beauty parlor, Merry-Pat's Kut-n-Kurl, so she could have all the permanents she wanted. This new one had turned her hair into real tight little circles flat to her head with skull showing.

"There's eats in the kitchen," Grandma said, "and plenty of clothes upstairs if you dig around for them. You know me. I save everything for a rainy day, unlike some." As she went past Mom, she turned for another look at her, as people often do. "You better stop down at the beauty parlor," Grandma Babcock told her. "That hair of yours needs work, Donna-Jo."

Then she tramped down the porch steps in her white

hospital shoes, waved her purse at us, and gunned off down Bates Gulch in her Duster. Brick and Bambi watched her go. "This proves what I've always suspected," Bambi said. "I'm adopted."

Mom was turning to Dad. "Donna-Jo?" she said. Her name is Beth.

"Honey," Dad said, looking his absolute tiredest, "it was all a long time ago. Practically forgotten."


Our first Hickory Fork day at Grandma's house is kind of a blur. Oh, there were clues, right from the beginning, plenty of them. Dad remembered when the ripped-up fence out front had been white, with rambler roses, and when the mailbox was still on the post. In the house there was a boarded-up back window and three locks on the door to the cellar stairs. Grandma Babcock had shifted her refrigerator over to block the back door. Plenty of clues, but we were too new to know, and Dad was in a daze. He kept seeing the Hickory Fork of his memories, and it was going to take a lot for him to get over it.

He'd grown up here, but the house wasn't quite the size of our garage in Bel-Air, though there was an upstairs. Casing the place, Bambi appeared at the top of the stairs. "There must be some mistake," she said. "I can only find one bathroom."

"There is only one bathroom," Dad said.

"In that case I'm first." Bambi vanished, and we heard water running. From there she went to bed.

"She's going to try to sleep all the way through this experience," I told Mom.

"She slept a lot anyway," Mom said. "It's puberty."

"Well, I'm not going to sleep through puberty, when it happens to me," I said. "I'm going to stay up for it."

"We'll see," Mom said.

I moved a little closer to her. "Listen, Mom, how are we going to handle all this?" I said, meaning everything.

"I'm thinking," Mom said. "I'm thinking."

We spent the day exploring the house, and it was fun in a way. Dad's old room up under the eaves still had pennants on the walls and his vintage gym shoes. His letter sweater was still folded in a mothbally drawer. So were his little-boy clothes, small work shirts and denim pants, Brick's size. Dad pulled a glaring blue suit out of the closet. "I wore this to the senior prom," he said. It had a dry carnation in the buttonhole.

"Did you take Donna-Jo?" Mom inquired kindly.

". . . I may have," Dad said. "Yes."

"And what did *she* wear?" Mom asked.

"Who remembers?" Dad said. ". . . She had, like, feathers in her hair. And a silver-type dress. Cut low."

"Stunning," Mom murmured. "What flowers did you take her?"

"Who knows?" Dad said. "Orchids."

"Hmmm," Mom said. "Good choice."

By dinnertime—supper in Hickory Fork—you wouldn't have known us. I'd found a pair of bib overalls just exactly baggy enough. But then I have no fashion sense. With the overalls I wore an old thermal undershirt of Grandpa Babcock's. At least now my clothes moved when I did. Mom found a neat 1940s housedress with rickrack. Mom's a size 6, and, weirdly, Grandma Babcock must have been, once. Dad had raided his dad's tie collection and found this old hand-painted one with a hula girl wearing a grass skirt of movable fringe. He wore it with a work shirt. No matter what Dad wears, he's still going to look a lot like Kevin Costner. Brick looked like a lumberjack doll. It was all great gear. Do you know what all this would cost in a retro shop on Melrose?

Mom had pulled together a meal. She can cook when she has to. When Grandma Babcock blew in, she found us around the kitchen table, waiting. "You're beginning to look a little more like normal people," she said, noticing our clothes. She set down something heavy, covered with foil.

"Rosalee left this on the porch. She bakes a cake for every occasion, and you can't stop her."

Grandma whipped off the foil, and it could have been a cake. It was in a very strange shape, covered with coconut dyed brown. Decorating it was one licorice jelly bean, possibly an eye. Dad met its eye, then looked away.

"Son," Grandma said as she settled at the table, "you'll have to unload that van of yours and take it down to Bubba's gas-and-oil for the night."

"Mama, I can't afford to have that van serviced. I can just about keep gas in it."

"Just park it down there under Bubba's lights." Grandma darted a glance at Brick and me. "We'll say no more about it."

"Mama, you park your Duster out in the yard."

"Yeah, well, they've already got the radio out of it, and the spare." Grandma examined the kitchen ceiling. "And the backseat."

Bambi entered then, fresh from a day in bed. She was back in her Chanel and skirt. She'd rinsed out her panty hose. I know because when I went in the bathroom, they slapped me in the face. Now she was back in them. The sight of us stopped her cold. The bib overalls, the housedress, the hula skirt. She grabbed her forehead. "What is this? *Hee Haw*?"

Grandma looked her over. She seemed fascinated by how

Bambi's hair was all Vita Care Super Spritzed up. "She give you trouble?" Grandma asked Mom.

"She's at a difficult age," Mom murmured.

"But she was always like that," I offered.

Bambi flopped down and looked over the table. "Whatever this is," she said, "I don't eat it."

We worked out the sleeping arrangements. Bambi and I were to have the guest room. It only had one bed, but it was big enough if one of you isn't Bambi. There was a heated discussion about where Mom and Dad were to sleep. Grandma Babcock wanted them to take her room. "No, I want you two kids to have it," she said, putting her foot down. "I don't use it anyhow. I sleep down on the living-room couch."

Brick got Dad's room, but he roams at night. Brick does. Apparently exhausted, Bambi was asleep the minute her head hit the pillow. I was awake, listening to the house. I kept telling myself this was the place where Dad grew up, but I kept thinking about *Nightmare on Elm Street* instead. And I kept seeing these strange shapes in the cracks on the wall. Outside, tree branches scraped the aluminum siding.

Then something strange was standing at the door. A ghastly white blob that made the dark around it darker. Sort of a small gnome-shape. Brick.

I could tell he'd been wandering through all the rooms. I'd heard him. He's a curious kid. Now he was by the bed, trailing a long nightshirt. "Buffie?" he whispered. "You awake?"

"No."

"If you two don't shut up," Bambi said, "I'm going to hurt you." But she seemed to be talking in her sleep.

"Grandma Babcock packs heat," Brick whispered.

"What?"

"She does. She's asleep down on the couch with a twelve-gauge shotgun on her coffee table."

"You're kidding me."

"And a box of shells," Brick said. "What does it mean, Buffie?"

I wondered myself. "I guess it means we're really safe here, Brick. Right? It's like, back in Bel-Air we had an electronic alarm system. Here we've got Grandma." (And a back door blocked by her refrigerator.)

The next day all three of us enrolled at Hickory Fork Consolidated School.

# Chapter
# Three

*T*he battle about going to school in Hickory Fork had started the night before we went. At first, Bambi wasn't negotiating. "I'm calling Amber," she said.

Amber, remember, is Bambi's best friend back in Bel-Air. They were really close even though Amber didn't go to our school because she isn't in the performing arts. Nobody has identified Amber's gifts yet.

"Why?" Mom asked.

"I'll just let Amber know I'll be coming back to live at her house. The Armitages' limo can drop me at school every morning, and it'll be cool. A conference call to Amber, and I can be on a plane tomorrow."

"You can't," Mom said. "I happen to know that Amber's mother is at Betty Ford this minute."

"Her dad—"

"Her dad is married to Serena's mother now and lives at Malibu."

Bambi wavered.

"And besides," Mom said, "I know about that pool party at the Armitages' last spring, the one with the funny punch and the police."

This brought Bambi to the bargaining table. Dad was upstairs in his room, helping Brick work up a school wardrobe. So it was just Bambi and me, Mom and Grandma, around the kitchen table. Girl talk.

"I'm not setting foot in a new school without knowing what they wear," Bambi said.

"They don't look too dressy to me," Grandma remarked, flicking lint off her electric-blue pantsuit.

Bambi pushed back from the table. "I guess we'd better get down to that Penny-Pincher Val-U-Mart place. Is that the only store in town?"

"It is now," Grandma said.

"How late is it open?" Bambi hadn't shopped in two days and was developing a twitch.

"Nine o'clock," Grandma said, "if it isn't raining."

"We can't go to Penny-Pincher Val-U-Mart," Mom said. "We'll have to make do without."

I just sat there. I don't let Bambi fight my battles for me, usually. But I let her carry the ball this time. After all, there ought to be some advantage to being a younger sister, even Bambi's. Actually, I was just as worried as she was about a new school. Maybe more. "Be real," Bambi said to Mom. "People will think we're poor."

"We are," Mom said.

That may have been the first moment it dawned on Bambi and me. We'd never even met anybody poor before. Now we were. It was like looking down and noticing the floor isn't there anymore.

"Now we're poor," Mom said. "But we're still us."

Grandma Babcock pursed up her lips and nodded. She isn't an approving-type person, but for a moment she looked like she approved of Mom. Bambi blinked.

Dad enrolled the three of us in school the next morning. It was a walk down the hill to Bubba's gas-and-oil and a drive in the van up another hill.

Hickory Fork Consolidated was two corrugated iron structures, the grade school on the left, the high school and gym on the right with a breezeway between. Parking lot in front, football field behind. Basic. I'm not into auras, but there was an atmosphere hanging over that school I really didn't like. You could see it from here. Yellow school buses were pulling up. I think that was the point when Bambi realized it was a public school.

But I'll say this for her. She's a show-business kid. When she knows she has to, she'll hit her mark and say her lines.

As the school loomed up, she sighed and said, "Okay, Dad, what's my motivation for this?" She always says that when she's walking onto the set, and now she was applying it.

"Don't think of it as a star part, Bambi," Dad said. "Think of it as an ensemble performance. Watch for your cues and don't upstage anybody the first day."

I listened. So did Brick.

We started out seeing the principal, who'd gone to this school with Dad. Dad called him "Stretch." They'd lettered in everything. Dad was wearing his old gym shoes.

The principal was a big out-of-shape guy all in maroon polyester and sideburns. He was really glad to see Dad. They punched each other's arms for quite a while. "So you got tired of the high life out there in Tinsel Town and wanted to expose your kids to a real community, that about it, Bill?"

"More or less," Dad said.

You could tell that Dad was somewhat surprised that Stretch had ended up as principal, or in charge of anything. Now he was bragging to Dad about what a darned good little school they had going here in Hickory Fork. "Six un-defeated seasons in basketball, and nobody wants to play us in football. We've scared off most of the teams in the conference. The Pinetree Trace Panthers is the only team that'll play us on our own field. It's like the old days, Bill, but better."

Bells were ringing by now, so Stretch got down to business and said we'd have to have our records sent from our California schools.

Good luck there. They hadn't given us grades at the Stars of Tomorrow School for Girls in the Performing Arts. Instead, we had "anecdotal commentary." My last report card read:

> *Buffie remains poised in a pre–self-actualizing posture, about to make her grand jeté into the earlier adolescent improvisational experience.*

What Bambi's said is anybody's guess. Brick's school didn't keep records, and you could pay his tuition with Master-Card.

Anyway, we got sorted out, and school was starting. Dad reached down and gave us three hugs, three kisses. The big principal blushed and Dad saw.

"Look, Stretch," he said. "We're from California. We kiss a lot." The next thing I knew, we were in homeroom.

Brick got led off somewhere else. I was in the same homeroom as Bambi. You should have seen her face. But sixth, seventh, and almighty eighth were all in together. We were kind of crammed in, but this wasn't a school that wasted money on hiring a lot of teachers. Bambi sat as far from me as she could.

Even without any fashion sense I didn't think clothes were going to be a big issue here. There was enough bad plaid and dumb denim in this room to have a barn dance.

And another thing. This was our first school with boys. An enormous guy sat on my right. I mean he was massive. I couldn't believe it. He shaved. For all I knew, he could be married. He was pumped up beyond all reason. His chest was steel bands. It could be Schwarzenegger. I'd seen him before, with the other guy walking across the bridge yesterday. Indoors, he was bigger. But I must have been desperate for some human contact. I caught his eye.

"Buffie," I said, pointing to myself. "New in town."

"Bob," he said. "Born here."

You couldn't hear yourself think in homeroom, but his voice had changed, so he boomed. He stuck a hand the size of my head across the aisle for me to shake.

"Are you a practice teacher or something?"

He shook his head. His neck was bigger than my waist.

"My daddy redlined me. I'm sitting out another year in eighth grade to get my weight up for high-school football." He jerked his head in the direction of the high school.

"My daddy's the coach," Bob said. "Coach Wire. You probably met him this morning."

"We only met the principal."

"That's what I said," Bob replied.

"You mean the principal is the coach?"

"Aren't they always?"

"Yeah, we met . . . Stretch."

"They called Daddy 'Stretch' in high school. Now they call him Big Bob. I'm Little Bob."

Bob Wire.

I looked two rows over to see what Bambi was doing. She was doing her nails.

Half the morning got canceled, and we had an all-school pep rally. It was to kick off the football season and to work up some enthusiasm for the game with our deadly rivals, Pinetree Trace, those Panther people who were the only team willing to play us on our own field.

Everybody from first grade through twelfth assembled in the gym. I couldn't see Brick, but there was a section where some teachers were trying to protect the little kids. Bambi and I hadn't been in a school gym before. All they had at Stars of Tomorrow School was a room for dance practice, a hot tub, a tanning salon, and a juice bar. Now we were in this place with naked steel girders that looked like a hog shed. Smelled like one too.

Bambi made a beeline my way and was sticking to me like glue, which was a first. Frankly, I didn't mind. The place was more deafening than homeroom. All the high-school people were over in the stands across from us. A lot of black leather over there and knees sticking out of torn Levi's. But some color, too, nothing very subtle. And everybody in the place but us was wearing cowboy boots, including Stretch. On the high-school side there was a lot of activity—three separate fistfights. But they didn't clap and they didn't cheer. They just drummed their bootheels on the bleachers, like thunder, but meaner.

"What a bunch of barneys." Bambi sighed.

It was chaos, but there wasn't a lot of pep in their rally. One of the cheerleaders smoked. The crowd never settled down, but the pom-pom girls were out on the floor in school colors: Kelly-green and mustard. Bambi gagged.

"Gimme an *H!* Gimme an *I!* Gimme a *C!*
Gimme a *K*—"

"Gimme a break," Bambi muttered. "And *hick*'s the word."

"Show 'um the beef, show 'um the pork,
Let 'um know we're Hickory Fork!"

It looked like confetti, but people on the high-school side were throwing parts of textbooks out on the gym floor.

"And what is more,
Show 'um the score.
In yo' face,
Pinetree Trace!"

The team came on, lumbering through a big paper-covered hoop. Except for somebody named "Jeeter," you couldn't hear their names. But then everybody but us knew them. And it was true, they outweighed Little Bob Wire. Some of them were scarcely human.

The high-school side really got vicious when Coach Wire read off the names of opposing schools for the upcoming gridiron season. After Pinetree Trace, which they hated the most, we'd be playing Toad Suck, Oil Trough, Possum Trot, Natural Steps, Viny Grove, and Booger Holler.

The sound of drumming bootheels nearly drowned out these dreaded names, and the bleachers on the other side were a forest of fingers.

"Booger Holler?" Bambi said to me, white-faced.

The last one onto the gym floor was the school mascot. It was somebody in a really terrible costume: big, brown, black-eyed, and furry. And strangely, it wore penny loafers. The Hickory Fork mascot was a hedgehog.

"Well, that explains the shape of that cake Mrs. Rosalee Hatfield made," I said. Bambi groaned.

I'd been looking for Brick, and now I saw him, on our

side but down lower. He'd been looking for us, too, standing up on his bleacher and gazing around. When he saw us, he ran a little finger across his throat and mouthed words. *Is this a real school?*

# Chapter
# Four

**J**ust last Monday we'd been having lunch out on the lanai at the Stars of Tomorrow School: diet seltzer and designer pasta. Now, Thursday, we'd just been through the steam table at Hickory Fork Consolidated. The smart money packed their lunches from home and bought milk. Off our turf, Bambi and I ended up with mystery-meat sandwiches on white bread, mashed potatoes, and Jell-O that fought back. Lifting the lid of her sandwich, Bambi said, "Show me the beef, show me the pork."

Grade school ate first. We were at a long table of people who noticed us, but didn't say anything. I'd gone with the thermal shirt and bib overalls look. My fashion statement seemed to be Osh-Kosh B'Gosh.

Bambi was in Levi's from Dad's grade-school days and one of his dress shirts, loose and blousy, with the tails knotted over one hip. I'll say this for Bambi—she can look couture in anything. There was more food in the air of the lunchroom than on people's trays. I wouldn't have minded throwing my Jell-O, but I really didn't want to touch it.

We weren't getting anywhere with this meal. Then, suddenly, everybody jumped up and started leaving. Benches fell over, food flew. I was legally deaf by now anyway, and thought maybe a bell had rung. A girl had been sitting next to me. Now she was scrambling backward over the bench. Odd girl, and I never did catch her name. Her hair looked white. Either she was a very pale champagne blonde, or she'd been in sixth grade many years. "Did the bell ring?" I asked her.

"Hunh?"

"Did—The—Bell—Ring?"

"You foreign?"

"Yes. Did the bell ring?"

"Naw. But the high-school people come in here next. You don't want to be here then. You better get your b—"

"Thanks," I said, and we went.

At the Stars of Tomorrow School we'd called all our teachers by their first names. Sheena, Desmond, Monique, Dirk, Bettina, Lance—names like that. They were always calling in sick to go for auditions. Here we had one teacher for most subjects, though the sevens and eights wandered off for some of their classes. Her name was Miss Poole, and she was shaky on long division. She was a real wrung-out washcloth of a woman. Youngish, but teaching had aged her.

By the time we were doing English, I'd drifted to the back row. They were passing out workbook pages when I looked up to see Little Bob Wire sitting next to me. I don't know how I'd missed him. He was like Mount Rushmore.

"Hey, Bob," I said. "I thought you were repeating eighth grade. This is sixth, as far as I can tell."

"Yeah, well," he said, scratching his stubble, "basically I'm doing eighth grade again. But in English I'm still sixth." I was beginning to be concerned about his academic potential. But there was nothing wrong with his upper-arm development.

In a paragraph on the workbook page we were supposed to identify twelve misspelled words. I found thirteen. Next was a list of separate sentences, and we had to find the error in each. I was taking my time.

"They try to trick you on these," Bob remarked. "There's no mistake in sentence number four."

"Sure there is," I said. " 'The cattle were laying out in the pasture.' "

"That's what I mean," Bob said. "No problem there."

"But it ought to be 'The cattle were *lying* out in the pasture.' "

"Not around here," Bob said. "Around here, *lying* is tell-

ing a fib. Believe me. I've been through this workbook
three times. You ever read a story called 'The Red Pony'?"

I nodded.

"Get ready for it again."

I watched Bob work. I liked the way his ballpoint was
completely buried in his big fist. You could almost not see
his desk. He'd definitely pumped too much iron. But you
know something? I liked him. Okay, maybe he was the only
person who wanted to talk to me. Maybe he was even the
first boy I'd ever seen up this close. But anyway, I liked
him. We were coming to the end of the day. You could tell
because people were rolling up their workbook pages into
miniature guided missiles, then launching them. Here in
the back row you could talk in a normal voice, but Bob said,
whispering, "Is Buffie your real name?"

When I nodded, he squinted at me to make sure I wasn't
. . . fibbing. "It's a good name," he said politely, "except
around here it would be more like the name of a heifer. But
it's a good name." The bell rang, and Miss Poole disap-
peared behind a hail of workbook guided missiles, carpet-
bombing her.

I watched Bob hulk up the aisle, and I wondered. Maybe
his daddy was holding him back from high school until he
was big enough to cripple the entire Pinetree Trace team,
not to mention Booger Holler. But repeating sixth-grade
English? I'd already seen enough of this school to realize

nobody's that dumb. True, he didn't know how to use *lie* and *lay*, but then neither did Miss Poole. And by now he sure knew his way around "The Red Pony." Maybe Little Bob was holding himself back.

Halfway up the aisle he turned around and came back. "Say, listen, Buffie," he said quietly. "Most of the high-school people leave after lunch, if they have trucks. But anyway, don't hang around here after school. Go straight home. Get indoors." He glanced behind, to see that nobody was listening. "It was very nice making your acquaintance." Then he loomed off. His shoulders strained the seams of his big plaid shirt.

But we didn't go straight home after school. We should have.

At first I couldn't find Bambi. Then we couldn't find Brick. Finally he had to find us. All this time we were caught up in a wave of people all surging for the school buses. Were they just glad school was over, or were they running for their lives?

Anyway, one of us had to go to the rest room, probably Bambi. In the past if Brick was along, we'd just take him with us into the ladies' room. But now he was getting sensitive about this. "All right," I told him. "Wait here, and be here when we get back."

We got confused and went into the nearest girls' washroom, which happened to be on the high-school side. We knew the minute we got in there. A bunch of girls were hanging out around the sinks, eating pork rinds out of the same sack. They were high school, all right. They looked like a female mud-wrestling team. They may have been in here since lunch, waiting for cheerleading practice. A couple of them wore mustard-yellow pleated microskirts and tassels on their cowboy boots. I assume this was a uniform and not by choice.

There are times in life when you have every reason to run, but don't. We'd killed their conversation cold. About twelve eyes were on us. Bambi forgot why we were there and swerved to a mirror, checked on herself, ran some water. I followed.

In L.A. every girl we'd ever known had had her thighs waxed by ninth grade. This peer group weren't into regular bathing yet. You could tell they moved only in a pack, but one girl came up to Bambi. If she'd come up to me, I could have solved everything. I'd have fainted. She was wearing a sleeveless body shirt that read:

**BAD TO THE BONE**

and pedal pushers for the fuller figure. And a pair of gold-tone earrings the size of salad plates.

"New, arncha?" she said to Bambi. She was chewing something. Maybe gum, maybe not.

"New here," Bambi said, her eyes still on the mirror. Bambi can be cool. Bambi could get us killed.

A voice or two came out of the group. "Tell 'um, Winona-Fay."

Winona-Fay?

She gestured back at her bunch. In the mirror I noticed she had something on her arm. It could have been a birthmark, but it might have been a tattoo. It looked like a long-tailed rat, with whiskers. It didn't seem to be dirt. "I don't need to tell 'um they're in the wrong rest room. They've figured it out. They'll know better next time." She turned back to Bambi. "Hey, girl, how do you get your hair to stand up like that?"

"Lard," Bambi said. I felt sick.

"Naw," Winona-Fay said. "I tried that. You two city girls?"

"That's right," Bambi said. She hadn't bothered to bring makeup today. But she was running her little finger over the curve of her lip. Cool.

"I figured," Winona-Fay said. "The way you're dressed. That hair. I figured you-all were from the state capital."

There was an explosion then, from behind us. I'd been hearing them all day. And sounds like distant gunfire. But this was one of the doors to the stalls banging back, and echoing. I saw it all in the mirror. The fog of blue smoke in the stall, and this extra-tall girl stepped out of there, in plastic leather, ripped denim, white snakeskin boots. She was all black and white like an old movie. She had on a year's supply of eyeliner and about four pounds of matted hair, shoe-polish black. Pretty impressive and the scariest-looking girl I'd ever seen.

"Yikes," someone in the group said. "It's Big Tanya. We didn't know you were in there."

"That was the point," Big Tanya said. Her eyes raked the tops of their heads.

Bambi put one hand down on the sink to steady herself. Winona-Fay had whipped around, losing authority.

"No, they're not from the state capital," Big Tanya said. "They're from L.A. Back off, Winona-Fay."

I couldn't go on seeing all this in the mirror. I turned around and sort of hung on the sink. Bambi turned slightly.

"Don't any of you tread-heads watch *Entertainment Tonight*?" Big Tanya asked the group. "These here are the Babcock girls, Biffy and Bimbo—something like that. Their dad was a big deal in Teevee Land until they run him out of Hollywood. Their dad's all washed up in show business, so they washed up here."

Something went through Bambi. Even I felt it. She was standing taller too. True, the top of her Super Spritzed hair only came up to Big Tanya's collarbone. But Bambi was standing tall, and turning toward her now.

Big Tanya was up close. She was chewing something

because everybody chewed something here. Her hands were propped on her lanky hips. She had two press-on nails and eight bitten.

Then Bambi started doing her number. I couldn't believe she'd try that here, but she did. *She* looked *Big Tanya* over. She started with her hair, really trying to figure it out. Then Bambi's eyes dropped down to that little scatter of acne under the white medicated makeup on Big Tanya's forehead. Bambi skipped down over the nose and black mouth, then detoured to check out her earrings. In one ear Tanya was wearing three chrome shapes that dangled. Too polite to stare, I couldn't quite make them out. Mice? Rats? Creatures of some sort, with dainty little whiskers. In the other ear she had six holes, but only one earring. Some shape. Could it be a wedge of cheese? Surely not.

Bambi looked lower. She saw nothing of note about Big Tanya's chest and moved on. Big Tanya was wearing a sateen shirt, somewhat western. On it you could barely see embroidered, black on black, two letters—initials, but they couldn't be hers. They looked like *M. R.*

The shirt was jammed into black jeans. Lean though Tanya was, a narrow roll of flab was gathering at her middle. Pork rinds will do that. Bambi's cool gaze fell down ripped denim to Tanya's cowboy boots, which looked like they could coil up and strike.

It worked. I've seen Bambi do that on the set, just to put

somebody's timing out. ". . . What's your sign?" Tanya said, a moment off.

"Sagittarius," Bambi replied.

"Wuh?" That wasn't what Tanya meant.

"What's your colors?" Tanya asked her.

"I'm best in beige," Bambi said, "though white and navy work." She gestured down herself.

*Big Tanya doesn't mean that,* I was trying to say without moving my lips. *She doesn't mean that at all. What she means is—*

"You!" Tanya pivoted on a bootheel and snapped her fingers at the peer group. "Out."

They didn't even gang up at the door. They left single-file, orderly. A final flip of a mustard-yellow pleat, and they were out of there.

I couldn't hold back any longer, so I just burst out, "She's not talking about astrology, Bambi. She's not talking about *Sagittarius.* And she doesn't want to know how you coordinate your wardrobe. Forget beige. She's asking you what your *gang* sign is. She's asking you your *gang* colors. Ours. We're from L.A., so she thinks we're in a *gang.*"

Tanya nodded.

"What?" Bambi said. "Oh, for Pete's sake, we're from *Bel-Air.* We don't have gangs. We have fund-raisers." She twitched.

Tanya was dubious. She squinted at us until you couldn't see eye for eyeliner. "You two went to school out there?"

We nodded.

"Then if there's no gang, who runs the school?" But she was about ready to give up on us. She wiped her nose on her sateen sleeve and looked to the door for snoopers.

"Say listen, Bim—"

"Bambi," Bambi said.

"Tell me, you ever see any of those big stars out in L.A.? You know—like Vanilla Pudding?"

Vanilla Pudding?

Bambi stared. ". . . Oh, yeah, I see him around. At clubs. We've dated most of the New Kids on the Block. I have."

It was a fib, to put it mildly, but when Bambi tells one, she goes flat out.

Tanya's eyes glazed over, but it passed. "Okay, this is the setup. As long as you're here, be aware. Right? We've got a gang running things here at Hickory Fork. I'm talking the school. I'm talking the town. I'm talking total."

"What's your colors?" I asked, playing along.

"Hey, you in the bib overalls—you don't interrupt. But black, what else?" Tanya looked down herself. "We've got a pretty darn good bunch of homeboys and homewomen."

"What's your sign?"

Tanya gave me a dangerous look. "If you're not in the gang, you don't know the sign. You're not in the gang."

I shrank. Bambi listened.

"We don't take anybody lower than high school. We got no use for wannabes. So I shouldn't even be wasting my time with you two. But listen up. You're new, so I'm doing you a favor. Keep your heads down and your noses clean. If you see anything, you don't say. If you say, I hear." Big Tanya made a fist.

"Question," I said.

"What?"

"How many gangs are there in this school?"

Tanya's eyes bugged, and her black mouth smirked. "What kind of a question is that? One gang. Ours. We wouldn't let another gang on our, like, turf. We'd nuke 'um. We'd smoke 'um."

"I see," I said. "What's the name of the gang?"

"Name?" Big Tanya was not a lightning-quick thinker.

I nodded. "Like 'Bloods' or 'Crips' or like that."

"It's a secret," she said. "Anyway, why worry about a name when we're the only game in town?"

"Then who do you go up against?" I said. "Whom."

Tanya's mouth made a clicking sound. She looked at the fluorescent ceiling fixture. "Where have you been all day? Don't they teach you anything in fifth grade?"

"Sixth."

"Fifth, sixth," Tanya said, disgusted. "We go up against teachers, the town. Look, as long as there are grown-ups, we've got enemies, right? You got to get the upper hand with these people, and you've got to keep it. Give adults an inch, and they'll walk all over you. Am I right? They'd run everything if they got the chance."

"Ah," I said. Bambi fidgeted, and yawned. She does that when she's stressed. Another minute of this and she'd be asleep on her feet.

"I got no more time for you people." Big Tanya headed for the door. She wore a chain-link belt and cleats on her bootheels, so she clanked. "You're new, but now you know. And here's a hint. Forget where you came from. None of that Bel-Air stuff works around here. We decide what works." She made her exit humming a tune that may have been "U Can't Touch This."

Then she was gone. Without washing her hands.

"Yikes," Bambi said. "Who's *her* agent?"

When we figured the coast was clear, we left too. Brick was where we'd left him, like a little fireplug. "Did you see a tall girl," Bambi asked him, "all in black with really bad hair?" Brick pointed to the parking lot.

On legs like black scissors Big Tanya was climbing up into the cab of a truck, with a huge guy in a cap at the wheel. From here he looked like the guy who had crossed the bridge with Little Bob yesterday. When Tanya banged the door shut, you could read words painted on it:

## GRUBB'S GRUBS, MEALIE WORMS, FISHING TACKLE & HUNTERS' SUPPLIES

They tooled off.

Bambi's dander was up. It hadn't been a great day even before Tanya. "If we had a cellular phone in that dumb van of ours, I'd be on the wire to Amber *this minute.*"

We were walking now. Bambi doesn't walk, but I thought she could use some fresh air. Besides, how else were we supposed to get back to Grandma Babcock's? Not a limo in sight.

"You'd better forget about going to live at Amber's," I said. "You remember Mom's reasons."

Bambi simmered.

"Besides, you wouldn't want to leave Brick and me in this dump, would you?"

"Try me," Bambi said. But she glanced down at Brick. He hadn't had a good day, either, and it showed.

It was downhill all the way to downtown. And not a lot there when we came to the paved part. Bubba's gas-and-oil, a boarded-up S & L, a muffler outlet, Grubb's Grubs, Mealie Worms, Fishing Tackle & Hunters' Supplies, a funeral parlor next to a body shop, Merry-Pat's Kut-n-Kurl beauty shop, and a burned-out 6-Ten. The town wasn't even big enough for a 7-Eleven.

We took the long way. I saw to that. Bambi still needed a lot of chilling out. Past the fork to the bridge a path dipped down to follow Water Moccasin Branch. We took that.

"Tomorrow's Friday," Bambi noted. "I can just about deal with that. I could even make it through next week, with a sick day. But I've got my limits. I mean, it isn't even a school. It isn't even a town. I'm not sure it's a state."

Brick had picked up a tree limb and trailed it along the path. Burrs worked into my thermal top. The air here wasn't visible like it is in L.A., but it was a gray day. Then ahead, down by the creek, I saw a glimmer of color. Two colors. Kelly-green and mustard-yellow.

Bambi saw. Brick dropped his limb. But there were branches to screen us. We moved ahead, keeping quiet.

The creek flowed around a big rock. Somebody was sitting up on it, chunking stones into the water. He wore a mustard-yellow and Kelly-green sweatshirt, and we could read on his back:

### HEDGEHOG 13

It was Dad.

He was still wearing the Armani slacks from Monday, pleated front. With them, his faded Hickory Fork Consolidated athletic department sweatshirt, and his old, beat-up gym shoes, Keds. He had a little pile of stones beside him, and he was pitching them into the brown water. Every once in a while, *plop*, and the creek swallowed another stone. Dad's face was as gray as the day. I almost didn't know him because he's always looked ahead, but not now.

We stood out of sight. Even Brick didn't run on to throw his arms around Dad's neck. The three of us stood there until the pile of stones next to Dad began to run out.

Then we backed off and headed home the other way around. Now we knew, even Bambi. We wouldn't be leaving Hickory Fork anytime soon.

Bambi stalked on ahead. It reminded me of when she walks on the set, and maybe she doesn't know her lines, but she's willing to wing it.

Brick was keeping up, at least with me. Just as we'd found Bates Gulch Road again, he motioned for me to bend down. "I hate that school, Buffie," he whispered. "Those people eat their own."

# *Chapter Five*

**W**hen Grandma Babcock's missing mailbox was in sight, Brick and I were practically leading Bambi by the hand. For one thing, she hadn't covered this much ground on foot since the last Bel-Air Charity Walkathon against Bulimia. For another, she was lost in thought.

"We've got to have some major change around here," she said.

"Meaning?"

"You saw Dad back there. He's been down before. Remember when CBS canceled *Little House in the 'Hood* after thirteen weeks when he thought it might outrun *Beverly Hills 90210?*"

"Down," Brick breathed, "way down."

"Dad's been down before, but now he's *out*. Think about that. We can't take this laying down. I mean lying. See? It's all getting to me. These people don't even speak English. If there's any chance at all that we're going to get stuck here, we're going to have to turn that school around."

"Fine," I said. "We'll just nuke Big Tanya and . . . smoke that gang she belongs to. We'll drop by Coach Wire's office in the morning and ask him to take the school back from the kids running it, and the town too. We'd be dead people, Bambi."

"Forget Coach Wire," Bambi said, half to herself. "Forget every grown-up in town. They don't even dare go out at night. It's like New York, or someplace. Grandma Babcock's as tough as take-out chicken, but even she sleeps with a shotgun." Bambi shook her head. "If anybody's going to clean up this town, we'll have to start the ball rolling."

What, us?

"You know what Dad always says in run-throughs and rehearsals: Go with your main strength." Bambi was up in my face now, and Brick was all ears. "So what do we have that people around here don't have?"

"Orthodontics?"

Bambi sighed. "We're from show business, right?"

But we were a long way from it by now, and besides—

"So we'll show 'um. One way or another."

I didn't see how.

With four locks on her front door Grandma Babcock had to let us in. It was one of her days off from Kut-n-Kurl. She and Mom had set up the sewing machine in the living room and were busy as bees. They were recycling every stitch in the house for our school wardrobes. Mom said she hadn't been out all day except to drop by Penny-Pincher Val-U-Mart to match some thread.

"You shopped without *me*?" Bambi gaped.

"Somehow I just couldn't see you in a store that sells septic tanks," Mom said.

I wasn't sure what Mom and Grandma Babcock thought of each other. It would have helped if Grandma stopped calling Mom "Donna-Jo." And Mom's eyes kept drifting over to the tight little ringlets of Grandma's permanent. Still, they were about to run the fan belt off the sewing machine. Mom can sew if she has to. In her early days she did all her own costumes, her own makeup, hair, everything.

She'd cut an old fleece-lined sweatshirt down the front, trimmed it with grosgrain ribbon, and added gold buttons from Grandma's button box. For Bambi.

"I'll say this for you," Grandma Babcock remarked to Mom. "You're handy with a needle. And it's a good thing I went with the buttonholer option on this machine."

"I've tailored some of Grandpa Babcock's shirts for you, Buffie," Mom said.

"He had a real nice sea-island cotton with French cuffs," Grandma recalled, "though come to think of it, I buried him in it."

"How was school?" Mom asked as if she probably didn't want to know.

"Don't ask," I said.

"Bummer," Brick said. "Way bummer."

Bambi was pirouetting around in her restyled sweatshirt top. It wouldn't have passed in Bel-Air, but here it looked like an Adolfo. She stopped in mid-twirl. "Where's Dad?" she asked.

Bambi does that sometimes. She'll ask an innocent question just to see who knows what. Mom looked uncertain. She was developing lines under her eyes, either from sewing or worry.

"Women sew, but men sulk," Grandma Babcock said. "If I know that boy, he's down at the crick, chunkin' rocks in. He'd go there as a kid, when he'd get low in his mind. He'd be down there chunkin' rocks every time he broke up with Donna-J—with somebody."

Mom rested her eyes a moment, then opened them. "I'm going to cut down some of Grandma Babcock's old slacks for you, Buffie," she said. "Way down. I'll have you out of those bib overalls yet."

"Great, Mom. But don't overachieve. Clotheswise, you can't go too far wrong at that school."

Bambi went on pirouetting around the room, but she was starting to plot. You could tell.

Dad came home later, trying to look like he'd been somewhere. Dinner was quiet. Dessert was strange. Grandma Babcock had frozen the rest of Mrs. Rosalee Hatfield's hedgehog cake. Instead, she served up her own Ritz cracker mock-apple pie. It was a real taste adventure.

Since it was after dark, Grandma had battened down her hatches. This town really did shut down tight at night. If Mrs. Hatfield had a cake to deliver, she left it on a porch somewhere before sundown and scampered home.

Bambi scraped her chair back. "How about going out for a while, Dad? We'll walk off some of Grandma's good pie, and you can show us the neighborhood."

"Whoa," Grandma said.

But Bambi made eye contact with her, their first. Sent her some kind of message. Grandma Babcock clammed up.

"That's a great idea," Dad said. "I'll show you kids all my old haunts." Brick, who was in Dad's lap, looked up and blinked. To Brick, *haunts* may have another meaning. Ghostbusters movies are his favorites.

Mom didn't go. She was wiped out either from a day of sewing or a day with Grandma Babcock. Bambi marched me to the front door, the only door not blocked by a refrigerator. We were starting to unlock all the locks while Dad went with Brick to find him a jacket.

Grandma came up behind us, speaking low. "I don't like you-all out there at night. Especially that little Brick. Can he run? You-all want to watch out and not depend on your dad. He remembers this town when it was . . . different. He doesn't—"

"That's the point," Bambi said. "He's going to have to find out things aren't the way they used to be."

"You want to be careful about messin' with people's memories," Grandma said. But she backed off when Brick came up in a miniwindbreaker. Dad was in his old HFC Hedgehog warm-up jacket.

Outdoors, it was too dark to see the collapsed fence, the post without a mailbox. Hickory Fork had had a few streetlights, but they'd been shot out. We started with stars. Dad pointed them out, a whole dome of sparkling stars in a black velvet night. The only way you can see any astronomy in L.A. is if you get concussed.

"We could amble downtown and then up to school," Dad said, starting down memory lane.

I took the initiative here. "Dad, we've had enough school for one day." We went the other direction, up Bates Gulch and through a hollow or two. Faint lights came from a few houses, dim flickers from people's TV's, mainly black-and-white.

Dad walked on ahead with Brick. This deep in the red-neck night Bambi held my hand. Tripping over clods in the dark, we were so far off our turf, I could have cried.

"This is where the town used to end," Dad said at a crossroads. From there on the houses looked new. They even had mailboxes, but no trees. Just the occasional satellite dish.

"Remember sidewalks?" Bambi muttered, stumping along on the shoulder of the road.

"Why are you talking so weird?" I asked her.

"Some of that Ritz cracker pie is still stuck to the roof of my mouth. Could you kill for some mango yogurt?"

I was beginning to wonder what this walk was supposed to prove when Dad said, "It's funny, but we could be lost."

It didn't seem funny to me.

"I thought we were on the road out to the mall, but I don't see it. So okay, the mall killed downtown, but it's not a bad facility for a town this size." He squinted into the dark ahead. So did Brick.

Ahead at the end of the road were low, boxy shapes on the horizon, dead black against starry black. They looked like empty warehouses, bunkers even.

"It couldn't be," Dad said. But it was. Walking on, we came to a shot-out sign:

### Richard Peck

## A HEARTY DOWN-HOME WELCOME TO
## HICKORY MALL
The County's Biggest and Only Full-Service
Shopping Experience

Weeds had grown up around it. The lights were dead behind the letters. But you could still read it. I'd have turned back then. There was nothing ahead but a blacked-out mall like an ancient ruin. Dad walked on, disoriented. Now it was creepy. Too quiet. Bambi's hand was cutting off the circulation in mine.

"I can't understand it." Dad pointed. "That used to be all parking lot right up to the Sears store." Now it looked like a field that some farmer had planted in blacktop. The store at the far end was a big cube of darkness. On top was a sign that read,

### EARS

"I know the economy's in a slump," Dad said, "but this is ridiculous."

We listened to the wind for a minute, and then I saw it. Up close to the jumble of black buildings was another shape. A truck with a big cab. Things were so quiet out here that you could hear the motor idling. The truck jerked into gear and began to move. Spooky, because its lights were off.

Bambi noticed. The truck moved like a beetle over blacktop. "Dad," she said, a warning. Now the truck was heading toward the exit.

It turned onto the road. The four of us would have been in the beam of its headlights, but the lights weren't on. Almost a ghost truck. I couldn't tell how far away it was. You can't tell at night. But it was coming at us.

Time stopped, and then Bambi and I moved. She jumped Dad, and I went for Brick. Bambi leapt practically higher than her own head. She lit on Dad's shoulders and clung there like a backpack. Taking him by surprise, she threw him off balance. Brick was easier. I made one swipe and had him. We all four rolled into the ditch. One thing Hickory Fork isn't short of is ditches.

The truck gunned by, blasting exhaust. I'd grabbed ground and bounced back up, though where I got this combat training, I don't know. Bel-Air? Hardly. I noticed a couple of things. The stars were out, remember. There were words on the truck's door. I couldn't read them all, just:

### GRUBB'S GRUBS, MEALIE

And the back of the truck, a big open-bed with stakes—it was full of heads. People in the back of the truck, a whole gang of them, silent, holding on. It was like a hayride from h—

"Bambi!" Dad said. "Get off my head. Where's Brick? What are we doing here? Buffie, are you okay?"

Fortunately it was a dry ditch. We climbed out. "Look." Bambi pointed back toward town. Down the road, red taillights flared. The truck had hit its brakes. *If they start backing up, we've had it,* I thought. Dad was checking Brick over for damage.

The truck had stopped in front of a house, by a mailbox. Then the taillights went dead as it moved on. It braked again in front of the next house. Taillights turned the road red again. As it stopped the second time, the first mailbox blew up. It was like the Fourth of July. The mailbox became a quick orange fireball, and you could hear shrapnel skidding. It was a long way off, but Dad grabbed for us all. Then the second mailbox went off with a bang as the truck moved on to the third. It was making a deposit in every mailbox, something more powerful than a cherry bomb.

Four more, and the truck was gone. People were coming to the doors of their houses, but not outside. Dad was dazed. "This is terrible. We ought to call the county seat and get the sheriff over here."

"Dad," I said, "do you know a family around here by the name of Grubb?"

"The Grubbs? Sure, they run the bait shop. I went to

school with Jeeter Grubb. He married one of the Calhoun sisters. In fact, a couple of them. Why?"

"That was their truck."

"Couldn't be." Dad brushed himself down. "Jeeter Grubb won the American Legion 'Why I Am an American' essay contest three years running when we were in high school."

"Any kids?" I asked.

"I don't know," Dad said. "Probably. Why?"


You should have seen Grandma Babcock's face when we got home. We hadn't seen ourselves until we got indoors. Straw and tufts were stuck all over Brick. He looked like a little scarecrow. Things like thistles were clinging to Dad's last sixty-dollar haircut. He'd torn his warm-up jacket, a big rip right between *Hedge* and *hog*. Nothing touches Bambi's hair. Even her barrette was in place, but my head felt like a briar patch.

Grandma stared. "Looks like you-all got put in the ditch."

Dad keeps a year-round tan, but now he was ashy pale. "Mama, what in the world happened to the mall? I know the economy's in a slump, but—"

"Wan't the economy," Grandma said through clenched teeth. "Economy around here never was worth a—"

"But, Mama, Hickory Fork Mall's shut up tighter than a drum, including—"

"Don't I know it," she said. "The Mono-Plex Cinema is no more."

Then Bambi, Brick, and I learned something we hadn't known before. Grandma Babcock had had a stake in Hickory Fork Mall. She'd held the caramel corn and Milk Duds franchise in the lobby of the mall's Mono-Plex Cinema, the only movie theater in the county. It had been a real money-maker. In a way, Grandma Babcock had been in show business too.

This was such a hard concept for Dad that he was clutching his head. That's where Bambi gets that.

"But, Mama, why didn't you tell me?"

"You weren't to know, son. You got your own troubles, and I have my pride. I used to."

"But what are you living on, Mama?" (What were we all living on, come to think of it?)

Grandma's eyes shifted behind her trifocals. "I got my Social Security, which is just enough to keep hungry on. Then Merry-Pat took me on down at the Kut-n-Kurl. I was lucky there."

Dad was close to a sob. "Mama, how much can you earn at Merry-Pat's beauty parlor?"

Grandma grew shifty. "Well, she can only use me a couple days in the week. I do maybe three permanents, a wash-

and-set once in a while, and a comb-out. Stingy tippers, too, around here. A real bunch of tight—"

"Oh, Mama," Dad moaned.

Bambi gave me a look. Her eyes glistened because things were pretty sad. But she was sending me a message. Dad was beginning to get the picture, part of it. He still wasn't ready to make the connection between the truck that put us in the ditch and the total destruction of Hickory Mall, and everything else. You have to lead adults by the hand.

I looked up to see Mom at the top of the stairs in a borrowed flannelette nightgown, hearing this.

Then Brick, another mouth to feed, walked over to Grandma, leaving a little trail of straw on the rug. He took her hand and looked up at her trifocals.

"It'll be all right, Grandma," he said. "We're here now."

# Chapter
## Six

School started with a bang. In homeroom Little Bob Wire tramped down the aisle, sat, and the desk collapsed under him. It was bound to happen. They were grade-school desks, and he was Hulk Hogan. He was sitting on the floor now, surrounded by kindling.

Nobody laughed. Are you kidding? Nobody lower than ninth grade laughs at anybody that big. The solid sound of Little Bob meeting the floor silenced even homeroom.

Miss Poole usually kept on the far side of her desk. But now she was here at the back of the room, bending over Bob. I was across the aisle, noticing how skinny she was, all around.

"Bob, sugar," she said, "that was quite a fall. Bless your heart, you just went down with a bang."

She was talking to him like he was a little kid—in fact hers—and he outweighed her, twice.

Looking up, Bob said, "I'll have the desk fixed, Jean—I mean Miss Poole."

*What's going on around here?* I wondered. *Little Bob calls his teacher by her first name?*

"Oh, that's all right, sugar," Miss Poole said. "The school's fixing to fall apart anyways." She gave him her own life-size chair, with arms, where he could sit for homeroom and English. It suited him better, though he filled it up too. And it was next to me.

You couldn't hear the announcements anyway, so I spent homeroom time creating a piece of artwork. Art won't be my major, but this was a simple drawing. I drew my version of a big mouse, a rat—whatever. I put a little gleam in its eye and got fairly fancy with the tail. Lower down I lettered in two letters, *M* and *R.* Since I wasn't sure about them, I added a question mark. I used black ink, of course.

When Little Bob was settled into his new chair, I folded the sheet once and handed it over to him. He flipped it open and froze, then wadded up the paper.

"That about it?" I asked him. "Is a rat their logo and *M* and *R* their name, or whatever?"

Something like a red rash was climbing up Bob's big neck. "Don't know what you're talking about, Buffie," he said, trying not to move his lips.

"Be real, Bob," I said. "Big Tanya has already collared Bambi and me in the rest room and given us a welcome.

They're the mouse people, or something, and they run the town. Let's be frank. Talk to me, Bob."

He's polite, but he wanted me off his case.

"It's just better not to see anything, Buffie. Or say anything."

"If you want to get along, go along. Is that about it, Bob?"

"That's about it," he whispered, staring straight ahead. "Anyway, that's high-school stuff. We're not there yet. As long as we're on the grade-school side, we're okay."

I'd have kept him talking, but we had a fire drill then, the first of two that day. Bells went crazy, and Jean Poole ran a distracted hand through her distracted hair. People climbed out of their desks, in no hurry.

"It's not a real fire drill," Bob said without thinking. "They just set off the alarm whenever they feel like it, or if there's going to be a math test."

"They?" I said. "The Mouse People who run everything, but we're not involved because we're not in high school yet? Then why do we have to go through this cockamamie fire drill?"

Bob turned away, flushing under his stubble. He pushed his way up the aisle, practically knocking Bambi over.


Bambi brought him up at lunch. If I'm having conversations with a guy before she's even met one, we're going to have to talk it over. We brought our own lunches today and bought milk.

"One thing came clear," I told Bambi. "Little Bob is playing dumb to stay in grade school. If he's redlined to get his weight up for football, that only keeps him in grade school this year. Bob's looking ahead. He's dropped all the way back to sixth-grade English. Though he has it memorized, he's planning to flunk it, just to extend his grade-school career."

"How could you possibly flunk anything in this school?" Bambi looked around at the lunch crowd.

"Well, exactly," I said. "But Miss Poole likes him, so maybe she plays along. And I see Bob's point. Why should you have to join organized crime just to go to high school?"

Bambi nodded. Dad had told her not to upstage anybody on the first day, but this was the second. She was wearing blusher and had brushed in some cheekbones on her otherwise somewhat chipmunky face. A touch of color on her lips too. Even when we'd been on the lam from L.A., she and Mom had come away with purses crammed with top-of-the-line toiletries. "And these mouse persons would make Bob join their gang, wouldn't they?" she said. "After all, he not only has the muscle, he's the son of Principal Coach Wire."

Bambi seemed to think that *Principal* was Mr. Wire's title and *Coach* was his first name. She's not athletic.

"I don't know if being the principal's son cuts much ice

with the gang," I said. "Did you see Coach Wire out on the field this morning, trying to pretend it was a real fire drill and that *he'd* rung the bell?"

"Not an Oscar-winning performance," Bambi said. Then it was time to evacuate the lunchroom to make way for the high-school people. Benches turned over. Unfinished lunches sailed toward trash cans. Cowboy boots pounded for the door. We caught a glimpse of Brick in a flying wedge of first-graders. It was enough to panic me, but Bambi has her dignity. She even took out a little purse mirror and checked her lightly tinted lips for crumbs. You'd think she was just winding down lunch at Hamburger Hamlet in Westwood.

*"Bambi,"* I said, on my feet, "do you want to get us mugged?"

Her barely nibbled lunch was still in front of her. "You run along," she remarked.

"But—" Then I took another look at her. She was wearing her new sweatshirt Adolfo, and the makeup put a couple of years on her. Her hair was five or six inches higher than she was. She could have been ninth grade. Even an underdeveloped tenth.

"You're not going to try to—"

"Why not?" she said. "I'd like to get a better fix on the high-school people, just to see what we're dealing with here."

"You might look old enough to be in high school, but they'll know you're not. They'll know you've been in grade school all day yesterday and this morning."

"No, they won't," she said. "Nobody in high school ever notices anybody younger."

"Winona-Fay spotted you yesterday, and you couldn't call her gifted."

"I'm in makeup today," Bambi said. "And I won't stand up unless I have to."

It was true. Somehow she looked taller sitting down.

"But Big Tanya—"

"I doubt if she does lunch in here. She's probably in the rest room smoking and monitoring the pork-rind eaters."

"But what if she isn't?"

"Then I'll run for my life. You'd better make your exit. I'll see you after school, or at the next fire drill, whichever."

The doors up by the steam table burst open, and there was the sound of a cattle drive. I exited then because I couldn't even pass for seventh grade, let alone high school.

I worried myself sick about Bambi until I saw her again at the afternoon fire drill, still alive. That bell rang when we were doing biology workbook sheets on ragweed. The first thing Miss Poole did was grab for her purse. In fact, several people grabbed for her purse. Out in the hall I happened to run into Little Bob and asked him if he'd like to go to the fire drill with me. When I really get started with guys, I'll

**71**

probably be too pushy. But he was so polite, it was almost like having a date for the prom.

You're not supposed to talk during fire drills, but you had to yell to be heard. "Say, listen, Bob, you know anybody in school named Grubb?"

"Sure, everybody does," he said, again without thinking. "Little Jeeter Grubb. He plays football. You saw him yesterday at the rally. Last year when he was only tenth grade, he put three Booger Holler players in the hospital. Two of them during the game, one after."

We were outdoors now, and Coach Wire was practically running laps, trying to line us up and keep us a safe distance from the high-school people. Actually, there weren't a lot of high-school people at this fire drill.

"You want to point out Little Jeeter to me, Bob?"

He craned his big neck. "Since they have football practice after school, Jeet's probably going to afternoon classes. That's him."

Jeet was hard to miss. He seemed to be wearing full football padding, but he wasn't. His head was shaved. He had a couple of people by the neck, going through their pockets.

And I'd seen him before, three times. At the pep rally, of course. Then in the truck with Big Tanya after school yesterday. And on the first morning when we were driving into town.

"A couple of days ago, weren't you walking to school with Jeet?" I asked Bob.

He nodded. "His truck was in the shop."

"Are you two friends?"

". . . Not exactly. Listen, Buffie, I wish you wouldn't—"

"I know, Bob, I know. But I'm new in town. I'm just trying to get acquainted."

"It'd be a lot better if you tried not to," he said, but in a low voice, concerned.

The fire drill broke up the afternoon, which was what it was meant to do. After school, when Bambi and Brick and I found each other, we should have cut out, but I couldn't move till I'd heard. "Okay," I said to her, "what happened at high-school lunch? Threats? Shakedowns? Give it to me straight."

"It was fine," she said. Bambi can be really blasé sometimes. "First of all, I found out that nobody in the gang eats in the lunchroom. Apparently it's not cool."

"Then why does the whole grade school run for its life?"

"Well, they're still high-school people, aren't they?"

"But you passed," I said. Bambi preened.

"I sat at a table of tenth-grade girls. And I improvised a whole new identity for myself. I'm a second-semester ninth-grade transfer from the state capital named Tammy-Lynn. They bought it. The bowheads did."

"Bowheads?"

"That's what they're called if they aren't in the gang, if they're girls. They actually do wear these bows in their hair. They thought my hair was from outer space."

"But what were they like?"

"They were okay. Sort of sweet and simple. It was like a Tupperware party, or something. Sad, too, in a way."

"How?"

"Well, their lives are pretty empty. I mean, look around you. And they can't even be cheerleaders because they're not in the gang. Big Tanya won't let you get near tryouts unless you're one of her homewomen, or whatever."

I sighed. Brick did too. He was listening.

It was time to get off school premises. The last yellow bus had gunned away. The team was drifting onto the field for practice, Neanderthals in big shorts. Miss Poole was out in the parking lot, puzzling over the two flat tires on her Ford Escort. We started strolling.

"The bowheads can't even shop, not since the gang shut down the mall," Bambi said. "All they have is that Penny-Pincher Val-U-Mart place, and even they don't consider that shopping. Every girl at the table was wearing the same blouse. It was like the nightmare of polyester. So the bowheads can't cheer, and they can't shop. For them it must be the land of the living dead."

We were halfway down the hill by then. Brick was carrying something in his hand, but it seemed kinder not to mention it. It was a piece of first-grader artwork, Hickory Fork style.

"What about high-school guys?" I asked Bambi. "What do they call guys who aren't in the gang?"

"Dweebs."

No need to mention that they couldn't play football if they weren't in the gang. So there you had it. We're talking about a school with three groups: bowheads, dweebs, and criminal mice. I could have cried.

We went straight home. We didn't want to detour past the creek in case Dad was down there on his rock again, still chunking gravel into the water. Before we got up Bates Gulch, Bambi and I finally had to notice Brick's artwork. It was a construction-paper hedgehog with a real button for an eye and glued-on macaroni for fur. He'd picked off most of the macaroni.

I didn't know what they'd have been doing by now in his L.A. school, Sandpile Alternative. They probably didn't rush into reading. But they'd be doing something more creative and state-of-the-art than macaroni hedgehogs. I didn't even like asking him what kind of day he'd had. But I eased into it.

"So, Brick, what's your teacher like? Is she nice?"

"Ms. Stottlemeyer?" he said. "She's all right. I think she's an old hippie. She makes her own goat cheese and irons her hair."

Ah.

"What did you do in school today?"

"We made these things." He held up the bald hedgehog. "And we had fire drills. But mostly we watched films. One on tadpoles, two Daffy Ducks, and a long one on World War Eleven."

That stopped us in our tracks. Even Bambi, whose mind was still on the bowheads. "World War Eleven?" we said.

Brick held up two little fingers.

Bambi clutched her forehead.

"Brick," I said, "it was World War *Two*. It's Roman numeral *two*, not the number *eleven*."

"That's what I thought too," Brick said, "but Ms. Stottlemeyer says eleven."

Bambi's breath was coming in gasps, from the walk and now this. "That does it," she muttered, and there was murder in her mutter.

Bambi was so stressed out that I thought she'd sleep right through the weekend, puberty style. On Saturday morning Mom gave Dad his first home haircut. Then when Merry-Pat called Grandma Babcock to work a half day at the Kut-n-Kurl, Mom went with her. What we were going to do with Dad, I didn't know. He was beginning to pace.

That afternoon I went in our room to wake up Bambi.

She was unconscious in the middle of the bed where she'd been all night. I just touched her, and she sat straight up and reached for my throat. I'd interrupted a dream where she and Amber Armitage get invited down to Laguna for a fraternity beach party.

"Dad wants to take another walk," I said to her when I could get a word in. "And it's daylight, so I guess it's safe."

I expected an argument from her, but she threw back the quilt and said, "Oh all right. But I need the sleep, and so do you."

"Bambi, you've slept sixteen hours straight."

"I don't care. We're going to be out late tonight, like really late."

"We are?"

"Yes, but shut up about it." Her eyes darted to the door, for snoopers. "And we can't take Brick, so we'll have to make a clean break." Her eyes darted to the window.

"What are we going to do, run away from home?"

Bambi sighed. "We've already done that," she said, thinking of Bel-Air.

So Dad and Bambi and Brick and I took another walk. There was color in the trees and a nip in the air. I dealt with the weather by pretending it was air-conditioning. What winter would be like in this four-season setting, I didn't even want to think about.

At the crossroads Dad took the turning away from the

mall. He urged Brick to take deep lungfuls of good country air and tried not to notice the roadside litter. Dad was still looking hard for something about Hickory Fork that matched his memories. A splintered sign read:

## TO THE BOY SCOUT CAMP

Bambi rolled her eyes at me.

It dawned on Dad that Brick had never toasted marshmallows. "It was great," Dad said. "We'd sit around the fire out at the camp and toast marshmallows and tell chain-saw stories. Stretch and Jeeter and Bubba and I and the whole troop. It was great."

Brick stumped along, holding Dad's hand and stepping over the empties that had been thrown out of cars.

"And we slept in tents," Dad said, in a dream. "In the mornings we'd roll up our sleeping bags and clean up the campsite, jump in the pond, then make a fire and cook our own breakfast."

Bambi shuddered.

The old Boy Scout camp was just ahead in a grove of trees, with the gate off its hinges. We'd come to the end of the road now. Dad had.

Past the gate along a leafy track, it was fairly nice. Dad's nostalgia was working overtime now. He swung Brick up on his shoulders, and they both took deep lungfuls. Dad's mood seemed to be getting to me. I thought I smelled a campfire, or anyway smoke. "The old campgrounds were just around that stand of trees," he said. Right about then I had the feeling we weren't alone.

When we stepped into a clearing, it was full of people. And they'd never been Boy Scouts. Dad stopped so short that Brick nearly somersaulted down his front. Bambi gasped. But we shook these people worse than they shook us. A bunch of grown-up guys with a lot of facial hair sat around a campfire. One look at us and they all flipped crooked little cigarettes into the flames. There were women there, too, and maybe a baby.

At first I thought they were filming on location. The men were all in dirty camouflage and sandals. The women wore tie-dyed and love beads. No tents, but there was a bunch of vintage Volkswagen vans pulled up in a circle and painted over with peace-sign graffiti. The vans had curtains and mood lamps at the windows and garbage around the doors, so they must be living in them. There was laundry on the line, but it didn't look laundered.

But now I was noticing Brick, up on Dad's shoulders. He'd put up a little hand and was waving at this woman wearing something hand-loomed over her tie-dyed.

"Hi, Ms. Stottlemeyer," Brick said.

# *Chapter Seven*

*I*t was the darkest part of night. Bambi and I were in bed but not fighting, or sleeping. For dessert Grandma Babcock had served up the last of the Ritz cracker mock-apple pie. It had us pinned to the mattress. Branches scraped the aluminum siding outside. Then Bambi threw back the quilt. We were both fully dressed, with scarves and yarn caps.

"Where—"

"Shut up," Bambi said, "until we get out of the house."

"How are we supposed to do that? Don't forget Grandma Babcock sleeps with a twelve-gauge. She'd pick us off before we got down the stairs. She wouldn't know it was us, and I'll bet she's a sharpshooter. Also what about all those locks on her front door?"

"The window," Bambi said. The window was over the kitchen porch roof, and there was a drainpipe. Even if Grandma heard us back there, she'd have to move the refrigerator to get to the door. Unless she fired through the kitchen window.

"Come on," Bambi said.

"We can't, not yet."

"Why not?"

"Brick. He roams at night. All over the house. He wouldn't be settled down by now. You'd know that if you weren't asleep the minute your head hits the pillow, usually."

Bambi twitched. "If he roams all over the house, why doesn't Grandma shoot *him*?"

"Since he found out she's packing heat, he keeps out of her range. But he roams. With our luck he'd catch us just going out the window. Or he'd find the bed empty and tell Mom and Dad. I know he's not a snitch. But the kid's upset enough already, just having to go to that school."

Right on cue a small gnome shape appeared at the door, in a nightshirt. "Why are you wearing those caps in bed?" it said.

"Shut up and come closer," Bambi breathed. Now he was beside the bed, and so curious that his eyes almost glowed in the dark.

"Look, Brick, Buffie and I are . . . older. We need more . . . freedom."

"Get a life," Brick said.

"Just tell him where we're going," I said. Besides, I wanted to know.

Bambi sighed. "Brick, that gang at school totaled the shopping mall. They terrorized the storekeepers, and they vandalized the place, so it went broke. Nobody goes there now."

"Every kid in first grade knows that," Brick said.

"Well, do you know why? Why would a gang of high-school people ruin the mall when it was the only thing going in this town anyway? Why would teenagers, of all people, nuke the only movie theater they'd ever been to?"

Brick thought. So did I. Then he said, "Because they want it for themselves? Like a big clubhouse?"

I hadn't thought of that.

"Bingo," Bambi said.

Brick rubbed his little chin in the gloom. "But why are you all dressed up in bed?"

"Because Buffie and I are going out to the mall and case the place."

"Whoa," I said.

"It's Saturday night, so the gang will be there. Where else? We're going to see them in action, get a fix on them. Find out what makes these retards tick."

"Whoa," I said.

I don't remember what Bambi told Brick to keep him quiet about this. I do remember going out the window and

Bambi getting all tangled up in a combination storm-and-screen. We crept across the yard and then across Mrs. Rosalee Hatfield's. We walked our feet off and finally we were on a road of bombed-out mailboxes. Not a light anywhere, and a cloud across the moon. If anything moved, we were both ready to hit the ditch.

"I don't see how infiltrating the mall changes anything," I said. "Unless it gets us killed. Is that your idea of a solution?" But Bambi stalked on. A sign read A HEARTY DOWN-HOME WELCOME TO . . .

The mall lurked on the horizon under the big EARS sign. I figured we'd be fine as long as a truck wasn't in the parking lot. We got closer, and there was a truck in the parking lot. "This is the tricky part," Bambi said as we tried to cross blacktop while imitating moving trees. We stopped twice to listen, but all I heard was my heart. Now we could read the truck's door: GRUBB'S GRUBS, MEALIE WORMS, etc.

Things were entirely too quiet. A moving moon skated reflectively across the truck's hood. The mall's main entrance was a big mouth, with a loose board over a kicked-in door. "I wonder if they're bright enough to post a guard," Bambi whispered.

"Let's not find out. Let's—"

But she edged up and flattened her back against the boards. She was playing one of her roles—urban girl guerrilla or something. Then she was gone, swallowed by the mall. My heart hammered. But I followed her inside.

We hadn't thought about a flashlight. In the blackness I reached out and hoped it was Bambi. Junk littered the floor, and something soft that could have been a former cat. The place was a minefield, but our eyes adjusted. We didn't find ourselves in the arms of a big mouse halfback standing guard, or a kill-crazy cheerleader.

The main mall area opened ahead of us. It was like a big jungle cave. Black neon twisted like vines. There'd been indoor trees growing down the middle, but they'd lost their leaves. Bare branches reached up awful hands.

Along the sides dead stores stood behind signs:

**ROCK-BOTTOM PRICES, GOING OUT OF
BUSINESS**

And lettered in Magic Marker beneath:

**YOU BETER BELEEVE IT**

"What we've got here is the end of the world," I whispered. Bambi moved ahead to find another wall to flatten against.

We took it a step at a time. I tried to remember where the front door had been. Along the blacked-out former stores you could tell what had been there. One smelled like pot-pourri and candle wax. Another gave out the sharp tang of man-made fabrics. The stench of a grease fire came from a ruin with golden arches. At an intersection a sickening sweet smell wafted from a place that still had its sign: CANDY CORN CORNER. Then a row of stove-in doors leading to the big EARS store and another sign: TAKE 50% OFF EVERYTHING IN SIGHT.

Bambi wavered. We were still like the last two left after an invasion of the pod people. But somewhere in this huge, shadowy silence every gang member in Hickory Fork was hanging out, maybe waiting. She ducked into EARS. The ceiling was lower. The place was darker. Movable shelving blocked the aisles.

"Where?" she murmured, perplexed.

"Why?" I murmured, scared to death.

"The old movie theater," she breathed.

"Too dark," I said, "and confusing. We can't find it. We'll get lost. There'll be no way out. We'll get caught. We—"

Bambi moved out.

We hugged walls and skipped silently past the empty sockets of stores. We learned to avoid fallen logs that turned out to be benches for tired shoppers. Now in a big circular space at the heart of the mall, something strange stretched up into the indoor night.

It was a tinder-dry Christmas tree, all its needles shed.

The skeleton of a tree. The mall must have gone belly up at Christmastime. On the branches big glass baubles shimmered, dead eyeballs with nothing to reflect. Hung somewhere in this darkness, a glitter sign read, like a warning: ONLY FOUR SHOPPING DAYS LEFT.

And beneath the sign a figure was standing.

Bambi froze. The mall was big enough inside to have its own weather. A breeze lifted the lighter garbage and redistributed it with a seaside sound. Night birds had found new nesting possibilities up in the high darkness. But was there enough of this natural night noise to cover ours?

We stood moving no muscles, willing our eyes to see better. The figure turned. It was chewing something, so it must be local. It was carrying a tire iron, so it must be a gang member.

He—she—whoever—moved. The guard was walking guard duty. It made a military corner and walked toward the far side of the mall, wheezing and clanking. Leatherette and chains, no doubt. Bambi's hand closed over my wrist. We moved on, behind its back.

The movie theater was down a dead end. We found it by following the stale scent of caramel corn and Milk Duds. The darkness was total here, like fuzz against your face. Above the kicked-in doors, though, we could make out the scattered letters:

## NOW S OWING TEENAG MUT NT NINJ

We slipped inside, onto carpet. We're from L.A. We know our way around a movie theater, and this one was one-horse. Ahead would be Grandma Babcock's former refreshment franchise. We could take for granted the big industrial popcorn maker, the long shelves of pilfered candy bars.

And we could hear them now—the gang inside the theater, a bootheel sound, muffled but in there. By instinct Bambi glided toward the stairs to the projection booth. We moved upward by Braille. In the little room at the top we saw vague light coming through the two little projection windows. A window apiece.

I was still scared, plenty. But the projection booth seemed as safe a place as any. Bambi's face went to one of the windows. Mine went to the other.

The gang was clustered in the seats down front, like an audience in a nightmare. When they'd ruined the mall, they probably hadn't realized there'd be no electricity. They must have been pretty lost without it. But they were doing their best to have something like a live show, sort of their idea of a school assembly. There were a couple of road flares for footlights, spitting hot light. Three or four audience people were holding flashlights beamed at center stage.

The cheerleaders were up there in front of a torn movie screen in parts of their costumes. Mustard-yellow pleated skirts with black Leatherette tops, and their usual grooming. A very tall figure, all leather-bound, stood at the edge of the stage, directing—Big Tanya.

They weren't doing cheers, quite. I couldn't decide what they were doing, exactly. They were kind of hip-hopping around and trying to clap in unison and chanting:

> "Who we are? Listen and we'll tell.
> We're the Mall Rats straight from—"

A thunder of bootheels from the audience rose in a roar. And now at last we knew the name of this gang.

> "We trashed the mall, we're tellin' it true.
> We trashed the school, and we'll trash you.
> We be trashin' all over the place.
> Next Saturday we'll trash Pinetree Trace."

Bambi groaned. "There is nothing more pathetic," she remarked, "than a bunch of hillbillies trying to do rap."

> "Tell it like it is, tell it like it wuz,
> We trash everything just becuz."

They got really ragged then. The cheerleader who smoked didn't really have enough wind to go on. Winona-Fay didn't know her left foot from her right. And a couple of the others outweighed Little Jeeter Grubb. But they rallied for their big finish:

> "And now tonight, in a little while,
> We be puttin' wimpy Justin on trial."

"Who in the world is wimpy Justin?" Bambi whispered.

"A trial?" I whispered back. "They're going to have a *trial*. Let's get out of here."

I'd have been halfway to Bel-Air except for Bambi. But what we were witnessing could cost us our lives, and that helped me concentrate. The stage went dark, and the audience got shifty. They were as restless as homeroom.

The flashlights went on again, and my heart stopped. The stage was full of football players, the varsity team. It was like a police lineup where everybody's guilty. Leather whined and hardware rattled. Then Little Jeeter Grubb made his entrance. His shaved head beamed back at the flashlights. He wore a black sleeveless T-shirt with white letters across the front, reading: ALLERGIC TO THE LAW.

He had a life-size hedgehog by the neck.

Bambi swallowed with a sound. I, for one, had never seen a hedgehog in handcuffs before. Its hind paws only grazed the stage as Jeet frog-marched it into the spotlights. If you can frog-march a hedgehog. In this light it looked like a real animal, and it had more rhythm than the cheerleaders. But it was somebody suited up, the same hedgehog mascot from the pep rally at school.

"Aw right, Justin," Little Jeeter bawled. "We know you're in there."

"Right," echoed Tanya from the wings.

The hedgehog—Justin—stood slumped, surrounded by the team-gang. Jeet made a big business of checking his leather pockets for the key to the handcuffs. He mugged a lot for the audience. They responded with dutiful bootheels. When he'd come up with the key and unlocked the handcuffs, the hedgehog rubbed its wrists and then pulled off its paws.

"Take it all off." Jeet sighed loudly.

"I just put in on," came the hedgehog's muffled voice. "You made me." But he started to unbutton his furry front. Bootheels drummed. Now his skin was in a puddle around his ankles. He was wearing a golf shirt and gray flannels.

He was a scrawny guy, but high-school size. Though he stepped out of his skin, he clung to his hedgehog head till the last minute. Jeet thumped it, and Justin took it off. I'd never seen him before, out of costume. He looked intelligent and worried and very pale. Fumbling in his flannels, he came up with glasses and put them on. They gleamed in the flashlight beams, and the entire team moved in on him, closer.

"Aw right, I call this here meeting back to order," Jeet said. Everybody more or less settled down. Jeet sounded a lot like the president of the student council as well as head rodent of the Mall Rats. "Night court's in session."

He checked out Justin, who was a third the size of anybody in sight. "The charge is pretty serious," Jeet said, scratching. "Impersonating a hedgehog at a school event."

Justin said, "But—"

"Technically speaking, a hedgehog, if we needed one, is a member of the cheerleading squad. All cheerleaders is Mall Rattettes, which means they're gang members *and* girls. Make that two charges."

"But—"

"I call as witness for the Mall Rat prosecution, Big Tanya." She stepped out of the wings, and a flashlight beam found her. Even her eyeliner looked mean.

"Big Tanya," Little Jeet said, "as head cheerleader, you ever hear of a cheerleader who wasn't no girl?" Even the question embarrassed the first-string players. They stubbed their boot toes and wouldn't look at each other.

"Never," Big Tanya said, "and I'd like to add—"

"Add it later, Tanya." Jeet waved her off the stage.

"But—"

"Aw right, Justin," Jeet said, making with a big sigh. "Have your say. Incriminate yourself."

"But I *was* a cheerleader at my last school," Justin blurted.

The team went beet-red.

"We had to be guys," Justin said. "It was a boys' school."

Catcalls from the audience. They'd have thrown caramel corn and Milk Duds if they'd had any. Winona-Fay got all the cheerleaders on their feet, and they shook their fists. Even the road flares hissed.

"I forgot to put you under oath, Justin," Jeet said, "but you're under oath."

"It's true."

"Justin, you ever watch any pro football on TV? They're all guys, but they got girls to lead their cheers. They bring 'um in. It's what girls is for."

Justin just stood there.

Jeet looked confused, which may be his natural state. "Aw right, you're not in that school anymore, right? So you just forget you ever . . . led any cheers or anything like that. That was wussy stuff, and you want to forget about it." The team wiped their noses on their sleeves and examined the floor. "You ever show up anywhere in that hedgehog suit again, and we'll make you eat it."

The crowd stirred.

"That don't clear up the other charge, though." This one

really had Jeet worried. He ran a hand over the slick dome of his head. "If the bowheads and dweebs find out a non–Mall Rat was out on the gym floor during a pep rally like he belonged there, it wouldn't look good. It's not nobody's school but ours. We got all the power they is, and we don't share."

Tanya popped out of the wings and by flare-light led the gang as they chanted:

> "We the Mall Rats. We decide.
> You can run, but you cain't hide. Yeah."

"The damage has been did, though," Jeet said sadly, waving Tanya back into the wings. "You wuz out on the gym floor, and people are going to put two and two together and figure you couldn't be no Mall Rat. The public picks up on these things." Jeet rubbed the back of his shaved neck. "Looks like we got no choice but to make you a Mall Rat, Justin."

"But—"

"You're sure not up to our standards. You're different, and different don't do here. But we got like an obligation to our membership."

"But I don't want in the gang."

The place went crazy. From the audience hands grabbed for Justin on the stage, and the team had to protect him.

"Sweat him!" the Mall Rats howled. "Get him!" I thought things would never settle down.

"Whoa, Justin," Jeet said over the roar. "It don't work like that. *You* want in the Mall Rats, and *we're* not sure we want you."

"But—"

"Okay, we haven't got all night. We've got a couple of miles' worth of mailboxes to see to. We got us some road signs to collect, a van with California plates to hot-wire, and a barn-burning. We got an agenda here. Here's how it is. We vote you in, and then you get initiated. Then if you live, you're in. After that, you don't never have to decide anything. We decide. All in favor of Justin being in the Mall Rats, though he don't get any privileges, say aye."

Big Tanya popped out of the wings again like a stork from a cuckoo clock. "Let's see those hands."

Everybody voted. They all put up their hands and gave what must have been their gang sign. Two fingers extended, index and pinkie. Rat's ears, no doubt.

"The ayes have it." Tanya spoke fast before Jeet waved her backstage again.

Justin stood there in the dead center of the stage. His glasses reflected the flashlight beams like dimes.

Beside me Bambi was wringing her hands. "Go with it, Justin," she pleaded under her breath. "Join, Justin."

"No, thanks," Justin said.

94

# Chapter Eight

*F*inally they were gone, and the silence was like music. Bambi and I had stood there numb in the projection booth until the gang had finished with Justin. They'd initiated him anyway. Now he wasn't moving. After that they'd trooped out right under our feet, still trying to rap in chorus:

> "On our boots we wear these cleats—
> Keeps the grown-ups off the streets.
>
> "We run everything just our way.
> Dweebs and bowheads got no say."

They echoed away through the hollow mall. Still, Bambi and I stood there. She hadn't taken her eyes off the stage, even through the worst of it. Now the road flares burned low. Justin lay there in a heap of his hedgehog suit. The head had rolled free. They'd left him handcuffed. Jeet had found another pair for Justin's ankles. The last lick they'd given him had sent his glasses flying off into the dark.

When we could picture them all tooling away in Jeeter's truck, we moved. First the stairs and then the lobby. Then we were running flat-out down the aisle toward the sputtering flares, jumping up on the stage. I nearly stepped on Justin's glasses. I grabbed them, though I didn't know if he'd ever need them now.

We were crouched over him. The flares made everything a sickly pink. Then he moved. His handcuffed hands twitched.

"I'm insured," he said clearly, "and I'd prefer a private room. My physician is Dr. Renneker, and I was crossing at the light. My mother is lunching at the club. You can contact my father at the Polo Lounge."

Bambi blinked. Her arm was around his shoulders, propping him up. His eyes opened. I slipped his glasses on and hooked them around his battered ears.

When he'd focused, he looked back and forth at both of us, but he couldn't place us. ". . . Bowheads?" he asked uncertainly.

"I'll forgive you that," Bambi said. "You could have brain damage."

He tried to shake the cobwebs out of his head. "Sorry," he said. "I don't believe we've met. I'm Justin Thyme." He brought up a hand to shake, but both hands came up. He stared at the handcuffs, and now he seemed to remember everything.

"I'm Bambi," Bambi said. "This is my sister, Buffie. She's a lot younger. We saw everything. We're like witnesses."

"Oh, no," Justin said. "I think we'll just go with the concept that nothing happened and you didn't see it." Already he was moving to stand up, before he realized his ankles were attached.

"I'll take care of that," Bambi said, tearing off her yarn cap and whipping the barrette out of her hair. And still her hair stood tall. Bambi can pick locks because she's always losing her keys. With the sharp end of the barrette she went to work on the handcuffs. The light was bad, but she's good. A few deft turns of the barrette, and Justin was massaging his free wrists. Then she went to work on his other end.

She worked at lightning speed because something else about Justin was on her mind. Mine too.

"Justin," she said as his penny loafers sprang free, "when you were still, like, in a daze, you said something funny."

"Really?" he said. "I never had much of a sense of humor before."

"Not that kind of funny. You said your mother was lunching at the club and your father was at the Polo Lounge."

"Did I? Well, they're obviously not. It's the middle of the night. Isn't it?"

"Justin," she said, "where on earth are you from?"

"L.A.," he said.

Bambi's head fell on one of his shoulders, and I heard her sob. My head fell on his other one.

We clung together there in the heart of the ruined mall. It was incredible. It was like entering a black hole in space and meeting another earthling. We all talked at once, through tears.

"But how long have you guys been here?" Justin asked us.

"Forever," Bambi said. "Since Wednesday night."

"I've been here since before school started." Justin sighed. "Since last summer. Look at me. I'm as pale as a tourist." He extended narrow arms, pink in this light. But his beach tan had long since faded.

"Look, are you really, honestly from L.A.?" Bambi said. Though Justin was sitting up, she'd kept her arm around his shoulders. He wasn't killer good-looking, but he looked good to us. "Really and truly from L.A.?"

"Do you want to take your stick down to the beach and get tubed, or would you just rather stay home and pouch-grovel?" Justin said. "Or if you're hungry, we could go out and grind."

"You're real!" Bambi shrieked, breathing in this authentic California talk. My eyes were stinging too. "Where do you go to school?" Bambi asked. "I mean, where did you?"

Justin raised one eyebrow, and so we knew right there.

"Ivy Prep," we all chorused, and he smiled aristocratically. Ivy Prep is only the preppiest school on earth in Hancock Park.

Of course he went there. His gray flannels were pleated and cuffed. The golf shirt was socially correct and accurately faded. He wore no socks with the penny loafers. Wire-rimmed glasses. "But what are you two doing here?" he wondered.

"Our dad had some mid- to high-level creative differences with his monetary mainstays, had to deleverage, and is now in a regrouping mode," Bambi explained. It was great to hear real conversation again. "Are your people in the Business?"

"Show business?" Justin tried not to look shocked. "No. Family money." Which figures for Ivy Prep.

"But why are you *here*?"

"My parents got media-blitzed by the back-to-the-earth ecology lobby. Suddenly a passive-solar Tudor in Brentwood didn't cut it for them. We had a fairly spectacular garage sale, reordered the entire L. L. Bean catalogue, and moved here to get in synch with seasonal rhythms."

"You moved to Hickory Fork for environmental reasons?" Bambi gaped. "It's like Chernobyl with chiggers."

"Not really Hickory Fork per se," Justin explained. "We bought a mountaintop with a ten-room log-and-stone about a mile and a half from the mall. The original plan was that we live off the land. But now Father's going for a heated pool. And we found we needed an alarm and security system quite a lot more high-tech than the one in L.A."

"You can say that again," I said, getting a word in. "Our grandma has a refrigerator plugging up her back door."

"It's not great," Justin said quietly. "I don't know where my SATs are going to come from."

"How's your mom taking it?" I said. "Our mom hates it here. You can tell."

"That's another thing," Justin said. "Mother left. When we first got here, she went out to get some rays and got poison oak instead and saw a snake. Now she's at the apartment we keep at the Pierre in New York. Actually, my father's there too. He said he was going to bring her back, but he's taking his time. I don't think this back-to-the-land business is working for either of them."

"You're stuck here by yourself?" I said.

"Well, the servants and I," he said. "I wish they'd keep an eye on me. I went out for a walk this evening, and the next thing I knew, I was bouncing along in a truck bed, bound and gagged."

Bambi couldn't believe it. "Ivy Prep. I'm like zonked. Were you truly a cheerleader?"

Justin climbed painfully to his feet. The bruising on his face and arms was beginning to show. He planted his penny loafers, clenched a fist, and went into his cheerleader mode:

"Onward, Ivy, and pull up your socks;
    Secure the field and clean their clocks.

"Pursue that team right back to their bus;
    In future years they'll be working for us."

So he was definitely the real thing. "I can't believe you could go from a real cheer like that," Bambi said, "to being a hedgehog."

"But it's so *boring* here," Justin moaned. "I could have passed for a dweeb. Nobody noticed I was wearing natural fibers. But then one day I found the hedgehog suit in a trunk in the band room and got carried away."

We were down to one flare now. Bambi gathered up the ruined hedgehog suit and folded it to carry. Justin was trying to massage away some lower back pain.

"Anyway," he said, "you've both been excellent. It would have taken me quite a while to hop home with my ankles handcuffed. Even if I could find my way out of here."

But it was time to go. Bambi bustled. "Buffie, bring the head," she snapped, meaning the hedgehog's.

"Why don't we just leave it?" Justin said. "You did happen to hear that if the Mall Rats see me in it again, I eat it."

But Bambi paid no attention. She seemed to think it might come in handy. You never know.

We could find our way out. We led and Justin followed. He hadn't seemed to notice anything when they'd carried him in. The huge skeleton of the Christmas tree in the central mall area amazed him. But we were moving right along. By now we were practically creatures of the night. When we slipped out past EARS into the parking lot and the night air hit us, it was like the first whiff of the sea on a beach day.

Out on the road we'd be going separate ways. It was almost morning, and everything was at its quietest. You had the idea that roosters were about to wake up.

"Well, anyway, it was good meeting you both." Justin shook our hands, preppie style. "We'd better not know each other at school. I believe I wasn't supposed to be saved. As Jeeter says, the public can put two and two together, even here. It's going to be a tense week anyway. You know what they've got planned for next weekend's game with Pinetree Trace."

"What?" we said.

"Did you hear how they opened their meeting tonight?" Justin went right into it, and it sounded really strange coming out of his mouth:

> "Pinetree Trace will crash and burn;
> Them dumb turkeys never learn.

"We got a message we can send;
They can't win with no tight end. Yeah."

"Honestly," Bambi said, "I mean, it's hardly language. What are they talking about?"

"Pinetree's the only team they think might beat them. So they're going to drop a net over Pinetree's star player, kidnap him, and bring him to the mall."

"You mean you were only, like, a dress rehearsal?" Bambi asked.

Justin nodded. "More or less. They've got it all worked out. They're bringing Pinetree's top Panther to the mall on Friday night, late. He'll be trussed up and held in a hostage situation till after the game Saturday afternoon. It's just their idea of good sportsmanship."

Bambi jerked her yarn cap down over her ears and stamped a foot. "This has all gone far enough. We should—"

But Justin put up a hand. "No, they've got this place sewed up. Actually, it's not that different from L.A. You know who's running the streets there."

Bambi twitched. "Please. We're from Bel-Air."

"Bel-Air?" Justin gaped. "You guys are Bel-Air?"

And true, we weren't exactly dressed for the part.

"Incredible. I can't picture Bel-Air people saving anybody. Of course, the only Bel-Air girl I ever knew was a grommety little wannabe named Amber Armitage."

Bambi's jaw dropped, but she got it back. Amber, don't forget, is her best friend till death when they're speaking. And *grommet* is an L.A. word for somebody who's preteen but won't admit it. I smiled.

We said our good-byes then, after Justin told us one more time that we were both excellent. Then he turned back to say, "I take it you're not driving."

Bambi, who's three weeks younger than Amber, isn't even close to a learner's permit, but she admitted it.

"I mean permanently," Justin said. "Weren't you there when Jeeter mentioned that hot-wiring a van with California plates is on their agenda tonight? I assume it's yours. We only have Volvos and an Infiniti."

I sighed, but Bambi said nothing. Then it was just the two of us stumping along the road back toward Bates Gulch. "We'll never get out of this place now," I muttered, gripping the hedgehog head and trying to keep up. "It just gets worse. Now we don't even have wheels. We'll grow old and die here, if the Mall Rats let us live. I'll marry Bob Wire and have twelve children and never go to another screening."

I was skipping to keep up with her, and my legs are longer than hers. "And how are we going to get back up the drainpipe and into the window of our room? It's going to be harder getting back than it was getting out, believe me. And we're carrying all this stuff, which I don't see the point of."

"Will you stop whining for two minutes?" Bambi barked. "You'll push me, and then I'll pull you, and you can throw the head on the porch roof. And who cares if they hot-wired our van? I'm glad. It's about time Dad woke up. I'm going public to Mom and Dad about this whole situation."

Bambi never goes public to Dad and especially Mom about anything, so I knew there were major changes ahead. She stalked on, just as a line of morning light began to dawn on Hickory Fork.

A pale gray ground fog shrouded our feet as we crossed Mrs. Rosalee Hatfield's yard. Then we were around behind our house. Dawn breezes rustled the autumn leaves, but otherwise the world was still asleep. The drainpipe looked slick. Our bedroom window with the bent combination storm-and-screen was still open, but far away.

Bambi pointed at the hedgehog head. I lobbed it up on the slanty porch roof, and it only rolled back as far as the gutter. Bambi made a wad out of the hedgehog suit, but it wouldn't throw right. It kept snagging on shingles and then coming back on our heads. She sighed and put it on. Now she looked like a shrunken, loose-skinned hedgehog in a yarn cap.

She pointed to her somewhat droopy behind. This meant I was to boost her up the drainpipe. It looked really slick, and she's bottom-heavy anyway. She scrambled up and at one point tried to stand on my head. I was grunting like a pig.

But pretty soon her hind paws were waving free in the air, and the major part of her was on the roof. I don't know how we thought we were going to handle the next part, even if it had worked.

She'd edged around up there and was looking back down at me. Actually, two heads were peering down, hers and the hedgehog's. She put an arm down. I don't know what I was supposed to do with it. I could get partway up the drainpipe on my own, with luck. But if I grabbed her hand, I'd pull her off the roof. There was nothing up there to hold her. It was pointless, and I panicked.

I started climbing up the drainpipe just a little faster than I was sliding down. Way up high, I could see Bambi's dangling hand in a furry sleeve. It was basically like a bad dream, and then it stopped. Everything did.

The explosion caught me halfway up. It all happened in slow motion: the long orange tongue of flame, the tinkle of breaking windowpane. Now the drainpipe and I were in space. We fell a long time into a flower bed. Though I couldn't fall any farther, I still had a good grip on the drainpipe. I smelled mint, but couldn't hear anything now and seemed to drift away into a deep, deep sleep. After all, it had been a long night.

I wasn't truly out except for a moment. And I got most of my hearing back. It was just that I didn't want to move. The drainpipe was cool, and the earth was soft. They don't call them flower beds for nothing.

There weren't any more flames and breaking glass—just a layer of smoke in the air above the fog. I looked around. Bambi was still up on the roof, sprawled near the gutter, and she seemed to be resting too. But this was all too peaceful to last.

Shrieks came from Mrs. Rosalee Hatfield's house. Then so did she, wearing what seemed to be a tent with ribbons. Quick on her feet, though. She thundered barefoot across her yard, vaulted a leaf bag, and kept coming. "Heaven help us," she gasped. "There's been gunplay over at Blanche's, and they're all dead."

Grandma Babcock herself, in men's pajamas, collided with Mrs. Hatfield, just about at the property line. Because of the refrigerator, Grandma had to come around from the front door, and there'd been all those locks. The twelve-gauge was still in her hand, smoking.

"Throw down that weapon, Blanche," Mrs. Hatfield screamed right in Grandma's ear. "There's been enough killing!"

I hadn't thought about being dead. I put up my head and looked around the drainpipe at Grandma.

"What in the Sam Hill," she said, and the shotgun clattered onto the ground.

Everything happened then, and I couldn't concentrate. I realized that Grandma had heard noises on her back porch. Probably the moment that hedgehog head hit the roof, Grandma was combat-ready and had the safety off the shotgun. Then she'd fired at random out the kitchen window, or what used to be the kitchen window.

Now the backyard seemed to fill up. Dad. Mom. I think I even caught a glimpse of Brick's sleepy face appearing at the upstairs window. Except for him they were all running into each other, and Mrs. Hatfield was whooping.

"Hi, Mom," I said. "Hi, Dad," which didn't seem adequate.

"Buffie, are you hit?" Mom said. They were all over me, trying to separate me from the drainpipe and get me out of the flower bed. They seemed to think I was out here alone. I wasn't about to take the rap for everything. When they got me on my feet, I pointed up to the porch roof. They all gasped.

Bambi was still sprawled up there. They no sooner saw her than the hedgehog head tipped over the gutter and fell to the ground. Mrs. Hatfield shrieked and covered her eyes.

"It's okay," I said. "It's the hedgehog's, not Bambi's."

I began to wonder what Bambi was doing up there in a dead faint. She'd been farther out of the line of fire than I was, and she hadn't ridden a drainpipe anywhere. Then I saw. Dad rushed over. Right on cue Bambi tumbled off the roof into his arms. Didn't bat an eye. Kept both of them almost closed. It was her usual good timing. She was putting a scare into everybody before the time for explanations came. And believe me, it came.

Dad carried her into the house. Mom would have carried me, but I thought it was too stagy. She was still half worried that I'd been riddled with buckshot. Then she did an odd thing. It was getting lighter, and she scanned the misty yard with wild eyes. When she saw the shotgun, she went over, grabbed it up, and broke it open to see that both barrels had fired. Then Mom took it by the barrels and began to turn. Her nightgown skirts twirled in the ground fog as she spun around and around. Then she let fly with the shotgun. It sailed all the way to the back of the property.

Grandma Babcock just stood there in her men's pajamas and the nightcap that protects her permanent. When she could get her jaw back, she said, "What in the Sam Hill come over you, Donna-Jo?"

# *Chapter Nine*

**A**t first there was some serious talk about punishing Bambi and me for going out our window to spend all night in a crime-ridden former mall. But Grandma Babcock's heart wasn't in it, since she'd nearly taken out two of her three grandchildren. Bambi mentioned that our van was gone, which distracted Dad. Mom listened to all our explanations with those new little worry lines by her eyes. Brick listened, too, without mentioning that he'd seen us leave.

Bambi and I, mostly Bambi, painted the whole picture for them. The school, the Mall Rats, the team, the mall, the activities in the former Mono-Plex Cinema, Justin, Jeet, Big Tanya, the forthcoming kidnapping—the total Hickory Fork experience.

Dad was stunned. Grandma said none of it surprised her any, and we could kiss the van good-bye. The county sheriff didn't make Hickory Fork calls. "Budget cutbacks," she said, "and besides, he's yellow."

After breakfast and explanations we adjourned to the living room to take a family meeting. "I think the first thing to do is give Stretch a call," Dad said. "Put him in the picture."

"Principal Coach Wire?" Bambi said. "Forget him, Dad. He doesn't want in the picture. He wants to win that game with Pinetree Trace just as much as the Mall Rats do. Maybe more."

"Bambi, he's the principal of the school," Dad said. "It's his job to—"

"Dad, please," Bambi said. "Trust me."

Dad sighed. "Bambi, how many times in the years ahead are you going to say those two words to me?"

But he didn't call Big Bob Wire, at least not then. Instead, he said he was going to call Jeeter Grubb down at the bait shop. "Big Jeeter, I suppose he is now. I can't believe he'd have a son who shaves his head and runs wild."

"Believe it," I murmured.

"Did I ever tell you that Jeeter Grubb—senior—won the American Legion 'Why I Am an American' essay contest three years in a—"

"You told us," we all said, even Mom.

Finally Dad cleared his head, located his center, and said, "What do we Babcocks do when we're not going anywhere and the chips are down?"

"A pilot?" Brick said.

We all looked at him, even Grandma. He was sitting in a corner of her sofa, picking at a needlepoint pillow and taking everything in.

Yes, that's what we do. A pilot. Suddenly everybody was talking, everybody having ideas. It was only a few days ago we were shooting a pilot. It wasn't like we'd gotten rusty or anything.

We started kicking around creative concepts. We'd need our old costumes, too, and dialogue, and maybe a revised script, and good timing. Lots of good timing. Dad even put together a storyboard. We had some props we could use. It was almost like the old days. You could feel a hint of the old L.A. hustle right here in Hickory Fork.

We worked up a countdown for the week ahead, including rehearsal time. It didn't take long for Grandma Babcock to get interested. She listened to us talking about the pilot we'd been filming in L.A. and how we could make that work here. When we dug out our costumes, she fingered them thoughtfully. "I could maybe pitch in somewheres and give you a hand," she remarked, "strictly backstage."

But you could tell she was hoping for at least a walk-on part. Show business is probably in our genes.

We'd need to keep our plans a secret, though we'd have to do some PR and publicity. I volunteered for that. We'd need more background too—local color stuff. Bambi said to leave that to her, and Justin.

I knew she'd work him in. I'd met a guy before she had, and Bambi was playing catch-up ball. We worked on our big top-secret production all Sunday and into the night. We were practically back in the Business again. We stood in front of Dad's storyboard with our arms around each other, everybody sharing and interrupting. Grandma too. It was our first good day since we'd come here.

Toward evening we found a cake out on the porch. Mrs. Hatfield had baked it for us because she has cakes for all occasions. "Knowing her," Grandma said, "it's probably in the shape of a shotgun." But it was just a regular angel food.

No doubt the Mall Rats were working on their own countdown in the week leading up to the big combination kidnapping and football game. They definitely kept busy because we had the usual ten fire drills in five days, and somebody blew up a toilet. And by Thursday every wall in school was spray-painted:

### PINTREE TRASE IS DAID MEET

Monday morning in homeroom Little Bob Wire was in his big chair next to me. "Hey, Buff," he said, friendly.

"Hey, Bob," I replied. When he'd settled in, I said,

"Which team do you favor in the big Pinetree Trace game Saturday?"

He flushed. He probably thought I was up to something, because I was. "I don't know," he muttered. "Us, I guess."

Homeroom was deafening. But I managed to say, "I don't know. I hear Pinetree's got a dynamite player."

Bob's big neck turned sunset colors, so he knew about the Mall Rat plan. Subtle, they're not.

"Number twenty-four," he said, "Jess Neverwood. He's good. He's their whole team. He even trains. Doesn't smoke, doesn't drink, doesn't chew much, steroid-free. I wouldn't mind playing football if I could be like . . ."

But Little Bob's voice trailed off and was lost in the din. Finally the bell must have rung, because Miss Poole plastered herself against the blackboard, and everybody barged out.

At least now we knew the name of the future kidnap victim: Pinetree's clean-cut Jess Neverwood.

Bambi said she wouldn't be seeing much of me at school that week. She was going to eat with the high-school people, doing her Tammy-Lynn-from-the-state-capital number. She said she needed a lot more details about the Mall Rat plan. But what was she going to pick up from bowheads and dweebs? Actually, she was trying to do lunch with Justin.

He kept such a low profile that he probably ate in his

locker. Bambi didn't nail him on the first day. When she did, he told her they couldn't talk anywhere public. She was willing to go private with him, after school. But he said he took the bus and tried to keep in a crowd all the way home.

Bambi can never take a hint. Finally she got him to agree to meet the two of us for lunch. Then she told me to find somewhere private on school property. The library sounded like a good place for complete emptiness, but Hickory Fork Consolidated didn't have a library. I went to Miss Poole.

It was about time the woman recognized me. She'd penciled me into her attendance book, but that was about it. Now I was going to ask to borrow her classroom for lunch hour.

Just before Wednesday lunch I cornered her. The crowd was going the other way. She was fishing a brown bag out of her desk drawer. When I asked her if Bambi and I could use her room for lunch, she said, "Sure, sugar." So I didn't know if she even knew my name yet. But she'd agree to anything.

"I don't want to put you out," I said.

"Lands, no," Miss Poole said. "Me and the principal generally have lunch in his office." She blushed.

*Me and the principal*—and the woman teaches English.

**115**

Bambi and I met in the empty classroom. When the coast was clear, Justin slipped in. I'd never seen him in daylight. He'd definitely lost his beach tan. The fluorescent lighting winked off his wire-rims, and he wore a button-down dress shirt, subtly striped.

"Where do you *get* shirts like that?" Bambi fingered his cuff. She was wearing a man's shirt too. Dad's.

"London," Justin said. "They have my measurements." He was looking around, nervous. "Listen, it's great to see you both, but why are we—"

"The kidnapping plot," Bambi said. "We—"

"The victim's going to be Jess Neverwood," I put in.

"*Everybody* knows that." Bambi sighed. "*Brick* probably knows that. We need details, a time frame, whatever you can find out, Justin."

He went paler. We'd all brought our lunches. His was heavy on the bean sprouts, tofu, and kiwi, with real blue-corn tortilla chips. I could have cried.

"Bambi, please," he said. "I don't know anything. I don't want to know anything. I'm trying to be the Invisible Man around here. I'm trying to fade into the woodwork."

"Not good enough, Justin," Bambi said. He had a jiggly Adam's apple, and it fascinated her. But Bambi was all business. Her designs on Justin were on hold through Saturday. "After all, you're a member of the gang, aren't you? You're a Mall Rat, officially."

"Bambi, what are you saying? They aren't even that happy about seeing me around school. They think I still ought to be handcuffed out at the mall. I'm no Mall R—"

"They initiated you, remember," she said. "You are definitely in their loop."

Justin's neck went red, though nothing like Little Bob's. "Bambi, what am I supposed to do? Shave my head and find somewhere to put a tattoo? All I want is to—"

"All you want is what we want—to break the back of these toxic turkeys. And we've got a plan, and you're part of it."

"What plan?" he said, one little bean sprout curling down from his pale lips. He didn't shave yet, but these things take time.

We'd drawn three desks together. His faced the door, and now the door was opening. I saw it from the corner of my eye. Justin reacted. He jumped straight out of his seat. Kiwi went everywhere. "Quick," he whispered, "give me your purses."

I'd left L.A. without one. Bambi had hers, of course, a little quilted leather number with braided strap, shoulder-length. He grabbed it up and in a completely new voice said, "Okay, that's five dollars today, and I'll need another five tomorrow."

He was actually dumping out Bambi's purse on a desk.

**117**

Her lip gloss rolled away. He was suddenly into the role of Mall Rat, shaking us down, doing the usual Mall Rat thing. So right there we knew that Justin was going to play a part in our plan.

But it wasn't a Mall Rat at the door to monitor us. It was Miss Poole returning. When she saw she was interrupting what amounted to a mugging, she said, "Oh, I beg your pardon, sugar," and left again, closing the door carefully behind her.

Justin handed Bambi's purse back to her and slumped into the desk. "What plan exactly?" he said, giving in.

So we told him.

That afternoon I saw my big chance. We were doing social studies or something. It was Miss Poole again, and Bob Wire was there. I never did figure out who taught what to whom. Bambi wasn't there. The seventh and eighth graders did either industrial arts or home ec that hour, though I couldn't picture Bambi in either place.

As usual, it took the class forever to settle down. Several things about lunch were still on my mind. One of them was Miss Poole and how she had her lunch with Little Bob's daddy in the principal's office. Struck me as odd.

"Tell me about your mom," I said across the aisle to Little Bob, just making conversation.

"She's gone," he said sadly.

"You mean really gone?" I said, pointing toward heaven.

He nodded. "To Texarkana. She said she wanted city life and ran off with an athletic-equipment salesman."

". . . So it's just you and Stre—your daddy?"

Bob nodded. "We're a couple of old bachelors. I wash out his socks for him. He's pretty busy running the school and coaching the teams."

"And dating Miss Poole?"

"I think they're sweet on one another," Little Bob confided. "Miss Poole's nice. She's real good about flunking me."

I thought. It was hard to picture mousy Miss Poole and Stretch as a twosome, but then this isn't exactly a town where you could film *Dating Game*.

Anyway, class was settling down somewhat. They were doing oral reports on local history. One girl got up to do one on her great-grandmother who during her lifetime had pickled over three tons of peaches. I don't think you actually had to write down your report. We saw several blown-up snapshots of a real old lady surrounded by jars and jars of pickled peaches.

Then a guy did a picture display of "Hickory Fork during the War." You could see the downtown the way it used to be. Actual stores, and a parade with floats and old cars, people in short skirts and square suits. World War Eleven, no doubt.

"What's your report on?" I muttered across to Bob.

"It's nothing too much," he said, modest as ever.

Nobody volunteered, but Miss Poole coaxed a few more reports out of people. One was pretty good, about somebody's Civil War ancestors, and two or three on quilts. You could begin to see that Hickory Fork had been a real place once.

Not all the reports were great. The dumbest girl in class gave one on "Outhouses and Septic Tanks Down through the Years." Then she wound it up by saying, "It wasn't until here lately our family could just go right into our own indoor bathroom and—"

"Thank you, April-Mae," Miss Poole said, running a hand through her hair. "Bob, honey, you want to get up and share with us?"

"Yes, ma'am," he lied, and lumbered to his feet. Manning the overhead projector, he said, "My report is called 'Hickory Fork Consolidated School in the Olden Days.'"

The olden days in this case seemed to be the 1960s. Bob's report came from his daddy's old school yearbook.

The first picture was the title page with a photo of the flagpole outside when there'd been a flower bed. The school itself showed new and blank without all the graffiti. And under it:

"Hickory Fork where our dreams began,
To live in the heart of each woman and
man,

"To our school we'll be true, whatever our
fate,
Dedicated to the class of 1968."

We saw a lot of school scenes in Bob's report: FFA, Debate Team, cheerleaders who didn't seem to be abusing any substances. It was amazing how clean everybody used to be around here.

Athletics took up most of the yearbook. A full-page picture of three good-looking guys and one great one, suited up for football. "This here is my daddy, Stretch Wire," Little Bob said, "and Mr. Jeeter Grubb and Mr. Bubba Breckenridge, and Mr. Bill Babcock, when they were lettering in everything." The great-looking one was Dad, of course. They stood with their helmets under their arms, looking skinny and squinting hopefully into the sunset. A lump appeared in my throat.

We went on through the yearbook, and it was the best report, up till then. Bob finished with another full-page picture of Dad in his blue suit and carnation and sideburns down to here. In his arms was a beautiful girl in a silvery dress with feathers in her hair. And underneath:

"Bill and Donna-Jo, both elected
'Best-looking' and 'Best All-Round' "

"This was probably the prom," Bob explained. "It's Buffie's dad with a date." Then he sat down, but he'd brought up my name.

Miss Poole grasped it. "Ah . . . Buffie, we'll excuse you from oral reporting since you're new and didn't get the assignment."

"I'm ready," I said, already on my feet. And I hoped I was, though I'd have to wing it.

I started up the aisle and hit my mark at the front of the room. This was the first time I'd looked the class in the face. They weren't too interested. Several were asleep.

"I don't have any visual aids," I said, which was true. "But I have an old story about Hickory Fork passed along by my grandmother." Which wasn't.

"It's probably a well-known piece of history around here," I said. "But I'll tell it anyway.

"It seems that outside town a mile or so there once lived a family named . . . Willoughby. I suppose they'd been a normal family at one time until a series of disasters hit them.

"They lived in a big old farmhouse that isn't there now. A father and mother, three kids, a couple of grandmothers. Good people, though they never mixed much.

"This Willoughby family had a little boy, couldn't have been more than five or six. He fell down their well. They hadn't even missed him until they lowered the bucket for some good fresh well water and brought up his bloated body instead."

Beside me Miss Poole stirred. A couple of sleepers out in the audience awoke.

"He was dead, of course," I explained. "The little Willoughby boy. They pumped the water out of him, but he was a goner. He could swim, so he'd been swimming in this little circle down at the bottom of the well. Screaming, of course, but nobody heard him. Swimming and screaming, screaming and swimming. Then he tired and drowned. He looked bad when they brought him up. All purple and green. His folks—Juanita and Wilbur Willoughby—were real sad. They couldn't even give his body up, so they buried him out in the back of their place."

I was beginning to get their attention now. Big Bob on the back row was all ears.

"The next to go was one of their daughters. She was not bad-looking, though a little chunky. Not a great student either." My eye scanned the classroom until it fell on April-Mae. She seemed as alert as she gets. "So this daughter dropped out of school to stay at home and help her mother with the chores.

"Until one day when she was helping her mother . . .

pickle some peaches. They were down in the cellar of the house. It was an old-fashioned cellar with an earth floor. Pretty damp. Pretty dark. Anyway, they were . . . pickling these peaches, and what this daughter didn't know was that just behind her head a long web was forming. Remember, it was dark down there."

The whole class was with me now.

"The web kept forming and getting more complicated— all these little silk threads weaving and weaving right behind this girl's head." I dropped my voice to make everybody lean forward.

"Then right behind her head the spider appeared. One of the bigger spiders ever sighted. It had black hairy legs and a body the size of a pullet egg. On that terrible body was the dreaded red hourglass mark. It was the mother of all black widow spiders."

You could have heard a pin drop in that room. Miss Poole's hand was reaching around the back of her own neck. People all down the rows were whipping around to look over their shoulders.

"All those spider legs moved now as the creature spun out more web, reaching nearer and nearer the girl's head. Nearer and nearer it came. Then the spider made its move. It swung on one silken strand across the dark air and was in the girl's hair." I stepped forward, and two girls in the front row yelped.

"Still," I said more softly, "the girl didn't realize that death was walking across her head on all its black hairy legs. She just went on pickling those peaches. Then the spider struck. The fatal thorn pierced the girl's scalp, and poured its poison straight into her brain."

"Oooooh," the class said.

"It took her a week to die, and by then she was crazy. Her head was the size of a watermelon, and what wasn't paralyzed was badly inflamed. Toward the end you couldn't look at her. She'd turned navy-blue before she died. They buried her out back, next to her bloated green brother."

A voice came from halfway back in the classroom: "Miss Poole, I'm *scared*."

"With two beloved children in the ground," I continued, "this family pinned all their hopes on their surviving daughter. She was beautiful, but headstrong. By the time she was in high school—here at Hickory Fork Consolidated—her parents began to think they were cursed and feared they'd lose her too. They locked her up a lot. She had to sneak out to go to her senior prom.

"She had an off-white dress with a pink sash, which she had to put on out in the . . . outhouse because her parents thought she was upstairs asleep in her room.

"Prom night was to be the best night of her life. In spite of her family's tragedies she was set on going to the prom like any other girl. She had a right to go to her prom."

"Yeah," two or three girls said.

"Anyway, she came out of the outhouse in her prom dress, carrying her shoes to keep them nice. She had to walk down the road to meet her date. It was a moonless night as that beautiful Willoughby girl walked along the rutted road in her prom dress, carrying her shoes, looking for the guy who was taking her to the prom."

I had them on the edge of their seats now.

"He was a little late. If he'd been on time, this would be a different story. So he was hurrying. Actually, I forgot to say, he was late because he'd stopped to buy a bottle of booze, which he was drinking in the cab of his truck. And he was driving with his lights off because he was coming to pick up this girl who wasn't supposed to be out. He roared along the road, driving with one hand. All of a sudden he sees this dim form looming up in front of the truck. Then he hears this thump, and he figures he's hit a . . . raccoon, or something.

"So he drives on, looking for the girl, but he doesn't see her."

I paused then. Beside me Miss Poole was hugging her elbows, and her eyes were huge. Nobody in the room was breathing.

"This guy—her date—gets all the way up to the farm-house, and still no girl. He doesn't know what to do. He kills the engine and climbs down out of the truck.

"Then he sees her. He'd hit her way back down the road, and the truck's dragged her all the way home. In her tattered off-white prom dress she falls out from under the fender where she's been wedged. Dead, of course. She's still holding her shoes."

I had them in the palm of my hand now. Two or three people had their hands over their mouths. Little Bob was on his feet at the back of the room.

"He picked up her broken body and started carrying her up to the farmhouse. When her parents opened the front door, they saw their last child being brought back from the prom she never went to, covered with road oil and blood. The Willoughbys buried her out back, too, along with the drowned brother and the spider case. Her remains were left in the remains of her prom dress."

"That's *awful*," Miss Poole whispered beside me.

"That's where the story should end, but it doesn't. Both the parents, Juanita and Wilbur, were driven mad by grief. They were a little peculiar anyway. They burned their farmhouse down, with themselves in it—and the two grandmothers too. They forgot they were upstairs."

I dropped my voice. "There's a curse on that land out there on the outskirts of Hickory Fork. Too much death on that condemned ground. Too much grief. Too much craziness. It's the land the Hickory Fork Mall was built on."

The class gasped.

"Yes." I nodded. "They shouldn't have built Hickory Fork Mall on that accursed ground. When they dug its foundations, they disturbed those unquiet graves. They let loose the spirits of the crazed and wronged!"

April-Mae burst into tears.

"Little wonder that the mall itself is only an abandoned ruin now. Little wonder that—"

But then we had a fire drill.

Still, I thought I'd put my point across. Let this rumor about the mall get passed around. Let it creep on little spider legs across to the high school.

During the fire drill Little Bob muttered to me, "That oral report you gave, Buffie. There wasn't anything to it. Was there?"

"Not really, Bob," I said. "But do me a favor and spread it around, will you?"

# Chapter
# Ten

*F*riday came and night fell. The Mall Rat plan had begun like clockwork, almost. The Rats' strike force had headed for Pinetree Trace in their truck. The Rattettes under Big Tanya's command stayed home and stood ready.

The gang knew Jess Neverwood's habits. After Pinetree's football practice they waylaid him on his way home. Their truck ran his into a ditch, and they dropped their net over him. In fact, they got two for the price of one because they also bagged Jess's girlfriend, a spunky Pinetree junior named Angel Bottoms.

There were no witnesses to this crime, none who were talking. Back came the Grubb bait-shop truck over the looping two-lane to Hickory Fork. Jess was bound and gagged in the truck bed. Three big Rats had to sit on Angel to keep her under control.

Now at nine-thirty, the truck eased into the mall parking lot. Another truck was parked there. It was the tow truck from Bubba's gas-and-oil, hidden where nobody saw, behind a Dumpster.

Lights off, Jeeter's truck slowed to a stop in front of the mall's big mouth of a front door. Mall Rattettes scurried from the weeds of the nearby fields. As they surrounded the truck, they were quieter than usual. Silently, the gang handed down the big bundle that was Jess Neverwood. They managed to drop him, hard, on blacktop. Then they handed down another bundle, not quite so big but thrashing around.

Big Tanya's voice broke the silence. "Who's *that*? Omigosh, is that Angel Bottoms? What did you bring *her* for?"

Though bound and gagged, Angel hissed.

Rats and Rattettes fell silent again, huddling in a tight bunch with their captives. For some reason nobody wanted to be first into the mall, though the whole place was quiet as a tomb.

Then Jeeter growled quietly, "Okay, Justin, lead the way. Since you're . . . a new member, you go first."

Justin was pushed ahead of the group. They'd brought only one flashlight and handed it up to him. Justin fumbled it, and it shattered on the pavement by the door. The group groaned. Having heard rumors, they were in no hurry to enter the mall. But a chill wind came up, rattling the corn in distant fields. "Now, Justin," Jeet said.

When they went into the mall, Little Jeeter and Big Tanya were neither first nor last. The group made no headway until somebody realized that Jess Neverwood's ankles were handcuffed. They unlocked them, but kept him bound and gagged.

"Don't unlock Angel," Tanya decreed. "Carry her."

They moved on, depending on Justin. He wore a modified version of Rat chic. His shirt collar didn't button down, and with his penny loafers he had on a pair of Levi's with tailored rips at the knees. Behind him the wheezing, clanking gang shuffled.

They moved like a black leather caterpillar across the cracked floors, making the turn at Candy Corn Corner. The black neon twisted like vines around them. It took most of the football team to keep from dropping Angel. She kicked and twisted and jabbed an elbow into an eye or two.

Every few steps Justin froze and looked from side to side, into the black caves of stores. He appeared to sense something different about the mall tonight. Then he'd move on, making the gang even jumpier. Yet the mall was even quieter than usual. No night birds. Something had seemed to warn them away.

The gang was coming up on that big round space at the heart of the mall when Justin stopped dead and threw out his arms. The Rat column stumbled to a stop. Even Angel hung suddenly motionless from eight football players. Justin looked back at the gang. His face would have been a ghastly pale blur. Then he pointed ahead past the ONLY FOUR SHOPPING DAYS LEFT sign to the tall Christmas tree.

It was the same tree reaching up tinder-dry into the gloom above. Yet—you had to look twice—among its blind baubles were dim lights, vague as fireflies. No cheery Christmas lights. No twinkle. Just pale winks of ghostly low-wattage light that made the tree more skeletal. It glowed without a noticeable power source.

"Not a good sign, actually," Justin said in a whisper to worry the Rats. But he led them on.

When they'd turned down the dead end to the Mono-Plex Cinema and you could feel the dark against your face, people were dropping back. Jeeter and Tanya were all the way at the rear.

Still, she was whispering furiously to him, "I don't see why you had to kidnap Angel too. That wasn't the deal, Jeeter, and you know it."

And Jeeter was saying, "Aw, Tanya, we had to bring her. She's like a witness, and she's got a big mouth if you don't gag her. Honest, honey, she don't mean nothing to me."

But Justin flung out his nearly invisible arms to stop them all just under the TEENAG MUT NT NINJ sign. Overpowering all the stale smells was the rich, full-bodied scent of hot buttered popcorn wafting from the lobby. Everybody got a whiff. It was amazing how scary this good smell was, because it shouldn't have been there at all.

"Where's it *coming* from?" some Rat whispered. Actually it was coming from the popcorn machine in Grandma Babcock's former franchise. But the peer group stood silent, waiting for Justin's answer. He had them right where he wanted them by now.

"I can't account for the popcorn smell," he said. "But you may have heard about that Willoughby family whose dead children are all buried under the mall. On the prom night when their daughter's date ran her down, they were popping corn in their kitchen. It was probably right around here somewhere. That was before they burned the house and the grandmothers down."

The gang muttered and shuffled. Somebody tried to laugh. Justin led them into the theater. He marched them down the aisle, figuring that when he bumped into the stage, the last stragglers at the rear would be inside. Then they realized nobody had brought a road flare.

It was like that moment when you're touring a cave, and they turn off the lights for a minute to let you know what complete darkness looks like—and how long a minute is. The Mall Rats had that minute. Then they heard the theater doors bang shut behind them, and echo.

The last people inside were probably Jeeter and Tanya. They'd have gladly saved themselves and maybe each other. But when they turned back to shoulder the doors open, they were locked and barred. Unseen hands were at work out in the lobby. Another pair of unseen hands were at work even among the Mall Rats right there in the theater. In the darkness nobody realized that two old clawlike hands had drawn the bound and gagged Jess Neverwood away from his confused captors.

Panic reigned all the way down the aisle. The Rats were scared speechless, though there was plenty of grunting. People stepped all over people, and those bootheels can hurt. In the hands of the milling football players Angel must have felt like she was on a rotisserie. Nobody missed Jess.

"Wait a minute," Justin's voice rang out clearly. "What's today's date?"

And a voice something like Justin's answered: "October eighteenth."

"Oh, no," Justin said, tragically but clearly, "not October eighteenth. That's the night the Willoughby family burned down their house. That's the one night of the year you don't want to be anywhere near here."

The aisle was silent as a grave, until Tanya spoke in a ghost of her usual bark. "This is like a joke, right?"

Then another voice said, "BE SEATED." And it was a voice nobody had ever heard before.

A mass of Rats had been trying to crawl over the seats anyway, though there was no hope of escape now. And they were used to doing what they were told. They groped into chairs. Team players stretched Angel out across their big knees.

"Yeah, everybody siddown," Jeeter bawled, but he spoke too late.

"If this is like a regular meeting," Tanya said, "I move that we—"

"Shut up, Tanya," Jeeter said.

They were all facing the stage, more or less. A dim glow pulsed brighter in front of curtains that hadn't been there before. The light never became bright, but it grew stronger on the swaying curtain. Hands—something—drew the curtain back.

A figure formed on the stage. Only a black shape and then an outline and then, perhaps, a woman.

From the fourth row a halfback whimpered.

The woman wore a long black preworn shroud, cut low in front and lightly singed at the hem. In life she'd been beautiful. Her long black hair looked real, though long buried.

As she raised her arms halfway to heaven, her batwing sleeves fell back to reveal the charred stumps where her hands had been. The entire football team lurched in their seats, and Angel revolved onto the floor.

Onstage, the stumps reached higher as if trying to force the lid of a closed coffin. Then the terrible figure spoke:

> "I am Juanita Willoughby,
> Burned to a crisp in '53."

She stared, dead-eyed, into the wings after her lost children, and her complexion was ashen, with actual ashes.

> "I am desperate now, for my children have
> died."

She pointed a stump at the audience.

> "You can run, but you can't hide."

She and the light faded, but before she completely vanished, it grew brighter somehow. Another figure stood beside her. It must have been old Farmer Willoughby, her husband. He wore black bib overalls and a black denim work shirt with grave stains. And his whole head made Freddy Krueger look like Tom Cruise.

In the same terrible voice that had said "BE SEATED," he spoke again:

> "I lit the match that set the fire
> That was to be our funeral pyre;

> "Who disturbs our graves will also burn;
> Some dumb turkeys never learn."

I personally wondered if this was going a little too far, but by now the Mall Rats were totally psyched. *I* was scared, and I knew better. I was also waiting for my cue, out there somewhere in the theater where no one had noticed I'd been all along.

Now the ghastly ghost of Juanita Willoughby was waving her stumps. In a voice that would stand your hair on end she moaned:

> "Oh, where is my baby, lost down the well?
> Oh, somebody save me from this terrible—"

"Here he comes, Ma," said Farmer Willoughby, pointing a blackened finger into the wings.

Sure enough, a shapeless shape appeared from stage right, down low. There was nothing human about it at first, only an irregular blob. Then it became somewhat childlike. A five-year-old, maybe a small six. It was green, and greener still around the lips. For some reason it had a beige hump on its back. It pulled itself across the stage on one elbow and two knees. As it dragged, it left a trail of dark slime behind.

You could hear swallowing all over the audience.

This was the child lost down the well. Swimming in those tight circles had somehow dislodged one of his eyes, because it hung way down his cheek. The lighting did the rest. I tell you the truth. After the first glance I couldn't look at him myself.

It was a former child that only a mother could love. But when Juanita's ghost saw him, she extended her stumps and spoke in a hollow voice:

> "Oh, speak to us, child; let us hear the dear
> sound
> Of the voice that we knew before you were
> drowned."

The little wet gnome-shape rested for a moment on an elbow. Then he looked up, training three sad eyes on his mother, and opened green lips to speak. But only about a pint of well water gurgled out instead.

In the audience there was the certain sound of somebody being sick.

Timing is everything, of course. While the little wet corpse was still spewing, something was forming upstage behind the heads of the three Willoughbys. Black and snaky like dead neon and then maybe a complicated design of ropes. You were aware of it before you really saw it. Then it became a kind of web, very dimly lit.

A little more light, and something seemed to hang captive in this nightmare net. Again there was no shape to it—just a free-form blob. Then it became a semihuman figure. Like a blue watermelon head wearing a peasant skirt. And needless to say, a real scene-stealer.

It tried to speak. But its head was so swollen that its features were all pulled tight. The mouth was only an oozing scar. But it had hands, entwined in the black web, twitching. The Willoughby ghost parents turned in slow motion to see it. Out in the audience people were ducking under their seats.

Onstage the spider girl tried to speak, but it was some hideous insect language. Her arms tried to work free of the web, and they were black, furry arms. Under her peasant skirt were extra legs, black and hairy. I couldn't look while the spider girl replayed her poisonous death for us. Not an easy act to follow.

In the midst of the stunned silence Big Tanya's voice was heard. "This isn't real, right? This is like TV . . . right?"

But then she knew it wasn't TV when I appeared in the aisle practically next to her elbow.

I was making my way, dragging a leg. A pinpoint light from somewhere found me and played over my blood-soaked off-white prom dress. My pink sash was tattered as if it might have been wrapped around a truck axle. For this part I even had a bosom. But only half a face. One half was all made up for the prom, with even false eyelashes. But the other half of my head was one big red wound where my date's truck had dragged me. With half a mouth I moaned like the lost. Take that, spider girl.

Except for the limp I seemed to float. Though I'd left half my mouth on a gravel road, I managed a strangled cry up to the Willoughbys on the stage.

> "Pity me, Papa. Pity me, Mom.
> I never lived to see the prom."

I was closer to the Rats than any Willoughby should be, and they were climbing over each other, but they lacked direction. I'd poured a half bottle of Grandma Babcock's Evening in Paris perfume over me, which seemed about right for a Hickory Fork prom. So I smelled to high heaven. That was the last straw for those Rats who hadn't already been sick.

I was down by the stage now with a truly eerie light on me. Though I wanted up on the stage with all my kinfolks, I had this gimpy leg. Finally, I hiked my skirt and threw the leg up on the stage. It was blood-red with loose blue veins, and it rolled away into the wings.

That got the biggest scream of the evening. I stayed down there for our big finish. The other Willoughbys turned to the audience. In the scariest collection of voices and gurgles you ever heard they moaned:

"Bad enough to build a mall upon our sacred soil,
    But then to trash the mall as well is enough to
    make us boil.

"We'll have revenge by whip or club—"

Then we all seemed to move nearer the audience.

"—Where's your leader, Jeeter Grubb?"

There was one more moment of stunned silence. Then near the back of the theater two hellacious red torches flamed up. Road flares, actually. Anybody with nerve enough to turn around saw that they were in the hands of two hideous crones wearing flame-red fright wigs. The two incinerated grandmothers of the Willoughby family, apparently. Though they made you think of cooked flesh, they smelled faintly of fresh popcorn.

The room went flickering pink, revealing Little Jeeter Grubb trying to get under his seat.

"Thur's Jeeter," said one of his faithful Rats, pointing him out.

Now Jeet was on his feet. The pink flare light played off his shaved head as he looked around for an exit.

"I wasn't the real leader," he yelled around a sob. "I was just fillin' in. Actually, it was Justin who led us in here. Actually, when you think about it, Tanya's really the—"

But another Rat broke in, "Look thur, the doors is opening." Sure enough, though the flares remained, propped on seats, the roasted grandmothers were gone. The doors to the lobby were opening, very slowly.

Jeet was the first one out. He skimmed the tops of the theater seats as if he were running for the touchdown of his life. A camera flash from somewhere caught him in midair. Tanya wasn't far behind. All the Mall Rats, unless you count Justin, were in full flight now, like a flock of big birds. The usual fistfights broke out at the door.

When they were gone, the silence was like music. Onstage the Willoughbys stood on their marks, staying in character. Then the little green drowned child rose up from his elbow. He pulled the extra eyeball off his cheek, spat out the rest of the well water, and in Brick's voice spoke:

> "Mess with the best,
> Die like the rest."

# *Chapter Eleven*

*T*hough the road flares still flickered, whiter light filled the theater. A little man with long sideburns, though thin on top, started down the aisle. He was Mr. Bubba Breckenridge of Bubba's gas-and-oil, the only citizen of Hickory Fork with his own portable generator. He was new at theatrical lighting, but not half bad.

Mom was still on her mark. Now she was lifting off her black fright wig and shaking out her blond Christie Brinkley hair. "I enjoyed that," she said. "I really felt Juanita's pain. You know, I think it's a better show now than it was as a pilot. We're getting the local color in and the bugs out."

Speaking of bugs, Bambi was out of her web now. "You'd better take off some of those legs, Bambi," Mom said. "You'll fall down and hurt yourself."

Mr. Breckenridge mounted the stage, stepping over my leg. He was grinning all over his face, though he kept his distance from Brick, who was still in his hump.

"You did a dynamite job, Bubba," Farmer Willoughby said, pulling off the customized Freddy Krueger mask. It was Dad underneath, of course.

"Glad to oblige," Mr. Breckenridge said. "To tell you the truth, I always was interested in show business. I ought to have went out to Hollywood with you, Bill." He grinned big, adding, "It done my heart good to scare the p—waddin' out of them kids. Nobody's done a thing about them lowlifes before, and they like to have tore up the town."

I wanted up on the stage, too, so they gave me a leg up, so to speak. Grandma Babcock and Mrs. Hatfield came down the aisle with fresh buttered popcorn for everybody. They'd taken off their matching flame wigs, though their permanents matched too. Between them was a guy. Grandma herself had plucked him from the Rats. Having worked in the Mono-Plex, Grandma can see in the dark. He was a 240-pound blond god with rope burns. Jess Neverwood.

This was really theater-in-the-round by now. Still out in his seat in the audience, Justin was swiveling back and forth to take everything in.

Grandma and Mrs. Hatfield were pleased with their performances as the doomed grandmothers. But Grandma Babcock said, "We got us some trouble here." She nodded at Jess, who was resting most of his weight on her.

It had been a big night for him. Jess had been as convinced as the Mall Rats that the Willoughbys were a bunch of mean ghosts. When he got this second look at us, his eyes were as big as his biceps. But it was dawning on him that we were human and he'd been saved.

Still, we had a problem. "Good evening, folks," he said, polite as Little Bob Wire, though surprised. "I'm much obliged to you—whoever you are. Or whatever."

I was peeling the wound off the side of my face. I must have looked a fright. He and the grandmothers were coming down the aisle slow. Jess was limping bad. I'd been limping too, but his limp was real.

Dad was completely out of character now, except for his all-black farmer costume. "Son," he said to Jess, "what's the matter?"

"When the Mall Rats rolled me off that truck," Jess said, "they put my knee out . . . sir." He was white around the lips and hurting. He was also looking all over the theater, kind of desperate. "Where's my Angel?"

At that point we Babcocks didn't know who his Angel was. But Justin shot out of his seat. "They grabbed his girl when they grabbed him," he said. "They must have taken her with them."

Jess froze.

But then we heard hissing under a row of theater seats. Justin vanished and seemed to be working his way under the rows like a preppie mole. "She's here," came his muffled voice. And she was, right where she'd rolled off the knees of the team. She was wedged under a seat, which had kept her from being trampled.

Though she outweighed Justin by a good twenty pounds, he got her on her feet. She was trussed up like a Christmas goose. Justin quickly ripped a big Band-Aid off her mouth, and you never heard such language.

It went on forever. You should have seen Brick's face. Angel finally wound down, saying, "I'll kill 'um. I'll kill every one of those Mall Rats. I'll waste that tacky Tanya. They are all *so Hickory Fork.*"

Angel was one assertive girl. She wore a vast sweatshirt, now wrinkled, that read:

## SEE YOU AT THE TRACTOR PULL

Justin was trying his best to untie her as Angel called over to Jess, "Honey, they've ruined your football career, but it's okay. I'm not just a gridiron groupie. I love you for the whole nine yards."

"Aw, Angel," Jess said.

By then the main drama was going on out in the theater. We Babcocks onstage were the audience. Bambi was prying off her blue watermelon head, trying to look her best for both Justin and Jess. She is so fickle.

I thought we'd done a pretty good night's work. The best

review we could have had was seeing those Rats hightailing it out of the theater on Jeeter's heels. Mr. Breckenridge was quicker than they were. He'd brought his camera and got a good shot of Jeet in flight.

But Dad wasn't happy. He'd dropped the Freddy mask and was helping Brick out of his hump. "Was it worth it?" Dad said. "I don't know. I wanted the parents here. I got the word out to the parents."

It was true. Dad had called Jeeter Grubb, Sr. He'd even called Principal Coach Wire. "I wanted them sitting there at the back of the theater. I wanted them to take charge of their kids. I wanted Stretch to take his school back. But not one of them showed up."

"Oh, well, Bill," Mr. Breckenridge said. "You know how parents is. They don't like to hear nothing if they can't do nothing. They dissolved the PTA. I expect I wouldn't be here myself if I'd had kids."

Dad gave Bubba a bleak look. Mom listened.

Also, the Mall Rats had put Jess Neverwood out of commission. By dropping him on his knee they had tomorrow's game sewed up even without holding him hostage. So it looked like they'd won again.

But then I had an idea of my own for Saturday's game. Smoothing out the tatters of my prom dress, I outlined it for them all. As Angel Bottoms listened to me, a wicked smile began to play across her face. Even Bambi thought it was worth a try.

It was a perfect blue-and-gold football afternoon for the big game. The stands were full at the only school event the parents attended. If there could be a great day in Hickory Fork, this was it. We Babcocks went, though we weren't up in the stands because it didn't look safe up there. We were down on the fifty-yard line. Dad wore his old Hedgehog 13 warm-up jacket. Justin was with us, so Bambi probably considered this a date.

The home team's supporters were feeling good. They'd heard that Jess Neverwood was in the medical unit over at Pinetree with a knee the size of a cantaloupe. So today they were there to see the Pinetree Panthers pulverized.

Pinetree's cheering section didn't hold out a lot of hope. But they'd driven over in their trucks, and were apparently heavily armed. It may have encouraged them to see the Hedgehogs run into each other as they surged out of the locker room. As captain Jeet was in the lead. But they didn't seem to be following him.

Hickory Fork didn't have it together, even the cheerleaders. Before Tanya knew what was happening, Angel Bottoms, the Pinetree cheerleaders' leader, had her maroon-and-gold Pantherettes out on the field and in formation. They went right into it:

> "Head 'um off, Pinetree,
> Kick 'um in the pants.
>
> "The Hedgehogs don't stand
> A GHOST of a chance."

They hit the word *ghost* hard, and their whole cheering section followed up with a long "Oooooh." A few of the Pinetree fans wore Freddy Krueger masks and fright wigs, so they'd heard the Hedgehogs had been shaken up by a weird supernatural experience. Pinetree rubbed it in:

> "Poke them Hedgehogs in the eyes,
> They're only Mall Rats in disguise.
>
> "Panthers gonna gitcha, gonna do our worst.
> Give up, goobers, you been CURSED."

A roar went up from the Pinetree people, while the Hickory Fork side simmered. Angel Bottoms had her Pantherettes shaking those pom-poms and kicking higher than Vegas showgirls.

Big Tanya finally got her cheerleaders out, but they'd had a hard night. Even their faces looked mustard and green:

"Show 'um the beef. . . ."

"Come on, girls," Tanya shrieked, "Get into it!"

"Show 'um the pork. . . ."

"Winona-Fay," Tanya howled, "face the stands, you *idiot*."

It was almost a relief when the game started, though it was more like a war, right from the moment when Hickory Fork won the toss. The basic Hedgehog strategy was to keep the ball in Jeeter's hands and generally sacrifice your own body to give him the glory. Instead, the ball went everywhere, and the Hedgehogs were blocking each other.

Jeet kept popping up from mounds of tangled bodies, screaming, "Hey, Hogs, here I am!" But too many Hogs were going wide and trying to score for themselves. Coach Wire was up and down the field like a fire drill. Still, we were ahead.

But Pinetree was doing its best without their number 24, Jess Neverwood, though they wouldn't play as dirty as

Hickory Fork. The clang of colliding helmets was sickening, and the field was muddying with blood. Brick had been up on Dad's shoulders to see everything. Now Dad lifted him down. "It's not football," Dad muttered. "It's just not football." You could tell that the Pinetree Panthers' coach agreed, and he wanted to win, bad. He happened to be Angel's dad, Coach "Bear" Bottoms.

By halftime the game looked like a wrap. Most of the Hickory Fork fans were staying on just to gloat. But the Hedgehogs had started overconfident. Now they were wearing themselves out. They'd been up late last night. They weren't really playing ball with Jeeter, and besides, the Pinetree cheerleaders kept up a chant:

"Spook 'um. Spook 'um. Spook 'um."

The Hedgehogs retaliated by rendering a Panther unconscious. They were still kicking him in the kidneys as he was being carried off. Somehow, at the beginning of the fourth quarter, the score was even, which kept the stands full.

Then the moment happened that was to make regional football history. Coming off the Panthers' bench as a replacement for the kidney case was the fabled number 24.

Everybody in both stands stood up, and the Pinetree side screamed. It was number 24—Jess Neverwood suited up, ankles wrapped, his helmet on, face greased black, his knees matching. A miracle. And just in case there was anybody who couldn't see the 24 in gold letters on his maroon back, he made a stylish little turn, and then he was in the game. His team took on new life, and the bootheels from the Hickory Fork stands drummed mean. Angel's girls did cartwheels, and in the Panthers' stands, Freddy Kruegers kissed each other.

A wobbly pass came out of nowhere into 24's sure grasp, which got the Panthers down to the Hedgehog thirty. He made some yardage, thanks to good Panther blocking. Hickory Fork called time out while Stretch and Jeeter screamed at each other and the other Hedgehogs. There was general spitting. Dad lowered his gaze. Mom hadn't been able to watch anything. Bambi kept her eye on Justin.

But it was already over. The Mall-Rats-by-night-Hedgehogs-by-day thought their best play had been to put Jess Neverwood away in advance. They hadn't thought as far as the game. Now here Jess was, fresh as a daisy and tearing up the field. The Hedgehogs broke out of their huddle, yelling audibles at each other. Play resumed. The ball was back in 24's hands, and there wasn't anybody within ten yards of him. There often wasn't.

In all he carried the ball twenty-two times in the fourth quarter, before the moment of truth. Time and again he either cut through the Hedgehogs like butter or vaulted over their dented helmets. He scored in the last two seconds of the game. It was over before people could believe it. Pinetree won.

There was the usual postgame pandemonium. First the goalposts came down, then the stands. We Babcocks and Justin were in a huddle of our own, to keep from being squashed. Big Tanya stomped off the field, mad as a wet hen. She just barely had her cheerleaders under control.

"And another thing, Winona-Fay," she snarled. "You looked about as bad as the team. Girl, you act like you got pom-poms for brains. And you always were so knock-kneed, you couldn't stop a pig in a ditch. I have a good mind to make you turn in your tassels and get off the squad."

"See if I care," Winona-Fay snapped back with hardly any fear in her face. "I got a notion to quit. What's the point of being a cheerleader if the team don't win?"

As the discouraged cheerleaders slumped past, Dad handed off Brick to Mom and vanished into the crowd toward number 24. The Panthers were about to carry him off the field on their big padded shoulders. Dad needed to get to him first. Dad's personal game plan was to spirit number 24 away before anybody ever discovered that he wasn't Jess Neverwood at all. He was Little Bob Wire, in disguise.

# Chapter
# Twelve

**O**n Monday the Mall Rats and their Rattettes called a skip day. The rumor was out that these tough cookies had been scared sick at the mall. Now the whole world knew they'd been creamed on the football field—at a home game. These were two body blows to their image, and they were off somewhere, rethinking their position.

So the high-school side looked a lot like the 1950s, populated entirely by bowheads and dweebs. They giggled nervously at the enlarged photos of Jeeter Grubb skimming over the theater seats of the former Mono-Plex Cinema. Mr. Bubba Breckenridge had driven halfway across the state for a Fotomat to provide the photography that blossomed on all the bulletin boards. Playing press agents, Bambi and Justin plastered the school with them.

It was a whole different school experience. Anybody could use the rest rooms, and we didn't have a fire drill all day. Better yet, nobody suspected Bambi and me of having a hand in all this. Heaven knows, Little Bob Wire wasn't talking. If the general public around school figured out that one of their own perennial eighth-graders had defeated their own team in the big game of the year, it might have confused them. Though it had tickled the Panthers' coach, "Bear" Bottoms, almost to death. He'd been heard to say that the Hickory Fork Hogs couldn't find their Astroturf with both hands.

"We'd better enjoy this while we can," I muttered to Bambi at lunch. "It won't last."

"What are you talking about?" she said.

"The Mall Rats will regroup. They may have seen through Jeeter as leader, and Tanya too. But what else have they got? What are they going to do now? Homework? Please."

"Dad says they've learned their lesson," Bambi remarked.

"Mom says they haven't," I replied.

"Dad says that even though the parents wouldn't come to the mall, they did come to the game. He says they saw it wasn't real football and that they'll insist on good sportsmanship from now on."

I sighed. Bambi is such a daddy's girl. Now she was staying on for high-school lunch. She was putting on eyeliner for Justin, who'd retired from the Rats. I picked up my tray to leave and said, "Actually, Bambi, you looked better as a blue watermelon with six legs," and left.

The school was in pretty good spirits that day, but Miss Poole wasn't. In English that afternoon, or maybe it was social studies, she said that her heart was so heavy that she had to share with us. She said that a school was only as good as its athletic teams, and that a principal's reputation depended on winning. Then she called for a moment of silence to mourn our loss to the Panthers.

Next to me Little Bob Wire swallowed hard and bowed his head.

On Tuesday the Mall Rats called their second skip day. It was rumored that on the night before, the Panther locker room had been torched. A van with California plates had been found on the front steps of Pinetree High School where somebody had tried to use it as a battering ram.

At our school the atmosphere continued to improve. Over on the high-school side, people were talking about bringing back FFA and the stamp collectors' club. But on Tuesday fate stepped in.

We knew something was up when the principal rocketed into Miss Poole's classroom in his sweat suit and flushed face. "Why, sugar," Miss Poole exclaimed. "What now?"

"Jean," he said, "get all your biggest kids over on the high-school side, pronto."

"But, sugar—"

"Now, Jean." He charged out again. We all blinked. Nobody had ever seen the principal in a classroom. Little Bob flinched at this sudden sight of his daddy.

Miss Poole rounded up all the sixes, sevens, and eights, except for the really underdeveloped. Needless to say, Little Bob made the cut. Before we knew it, we were across in the high school, being integrated with bowheads and dweebs. It was one sudden promotion. We found ourselves in a math class with Justin. So Bambi, Justin, Little Bob, and I were all in the same row, lined up like ducks. The class was having a unit called "Introducing Fractions." I hadn't a clue what we were doing here.

But before you could think, the door opened, and three old guys in suits walked in. They wore neckties, so they couldn't be local. Now they were counting heads.

I poked Little Bob. He'd been avoiding me because I'd been the one to call him up and convince him to begin his football career by defeating his daddy's team. He was pretty sure he'd done the right thing, but not completely. "Say, listen, Bob," I whispered directly into his ear. "What's going on?"

Here on the high-school side the desks were almost big enough for him. I looked over his massive shoulder to see his hands clenched together on the desk. The big knuckles were all skinned and bunged up from Saturday's game. He tried to hide them, but you could tell.

"They're from the state board of education, or somewhere like that," Bob mumbled. "They're counting heads because Hickory Fork Consolidated's enrollment's been declining. If we get too small, they'll shut down the high-school side and send the high-school people to another school."

"Like what other school?"

"Pinetree Trace."

I stared at the back of Bob's big red neck. And I noticed the head-counters up front were shaking their heads.

"Let me get this straight," I whispered. "Without the Mall Rats here it's not big enough to go on as its own high school?"

"With them here we're just barely big enough to keep going. That's why Daddy's sent us all over here to add to the numbers. But there's not enough of us."

"But even if the Rats are absent, they're officially on the school rolls, aren't they?"

Little Bob shrugged. "I don't think the state government has a lot of faith in Daddy's record-keeping."

Now I was grinning all over my face. If it hadn't been for our plans, the Mall Rats would have been in school today, running it, and being included in the head count. Now, they were liable to be sent over to the dreaded Pinetree Trace High School.

Little tears of pure pleasure were poking out of the sides

of my eyes. The Mall Rats would be nothing over at Pine-tree. Angel Bottoms wouldn't let Big Tanya near the Pantherettes. Coach Bottoms would keep Little Jeeter on the bench till the next century, whether or not Jess Neverwood got his knee back. Stretch Wire would be left behind as principal of a teamless grade school. I developed a bad case of the chuckles. And even now the rumor that the high school would be shut down was racing all over Hickory Fork.

I was feeling pretty good as Bambi, Brick, and I headed home that afternoon. I personally thought that the best thing you could do with Hickory Fork High School was to lock it up and throw away the key.

But I was wrong. Hickory Fork could live without their mall. They could even do without their mailboxes. They could even lose a football game every few years. But losing their high school was messing with people's memories.

Now we were passing quickly through downtown. We glanced in the window of Merry-Pat's Kut-n-Kurl to see Grandma Babcock in a pink nylon uniform giving some-body a comb-out. We looked again and saw Mom.

She was in pink nylon, too, zipper front. And she was working over a large woman. It stopped us cold. True, Mom had been going off to work with Grandma Babcock, but I didn't realize she'd hired on. Who has time to keep track of adults? Mom saw us and waved us inside.

Business at the Kut-n-Kurl had picked up. Mom gestured to a sign up over an old Clairol ad:

### AND NOW INTRODUCING BETH OF BEL-AIR FEATURING HOLLYWOOD-STYLE STYLING AND THE BEAUTY SECRETS OF THE STARS MAKEUP TIPS AVAILABLE

The chairs were full, and women were waiting, and they needed all the help they could get. Mom had put out a pot with cups and plates of cookies. The room was scented with a good California brand of herbal tea. She'd set a stage, for something.

On one side of the Kut-n-Kurl, Merry-Pat and Grandma Babcock were frying the hair of the older crowd in their usual permanents. Mom had a somewhat younger group on the other side, waiting for rinses, facials, and whole new eyebrows and jawlines. I read Bambi's mind. If anybody back in L.A. had known Mom was bending hair for a living, Bambi's status would be down the drain.

"Welcome to my new power base," Mom murmured to us. She turned and said to the room, "I'd like all you ladies to meet my children." The whole shop nodded and waved.

The town was actually a lot friendlier when you got to adults.

In an undertone Mom said, "Say pleased-to-meet-you. That's what they say."

"Pleased-to-meet-you," I said to a woman who had a dainty way of holding a plastic teacup. According to Mom she was the preacher's wife.

"Aren't you all sweet," she said to us. "I got me a little daughter in school too. Maybe you-all have met her. Winona-Fay?"

Bambi stared. Mom moved us on to two women enough alike to be twins, though they were only sisters. "Now, I can't quite get you ladies' names straight," Mom said.

"Oh, well, heck," said one of them. "Don't worry about our married names. Everybody just calls us the Calhoun sisters."

"Ah," said Mom. "Then which one of you is Little Jeeter Grubb's mother?"

"I am," said one, beaming proudly. "And sis here is his stepmom." They both beamed. We stared. Mom worked the room with us, and Brick shook hands with everybody.

The eyes of all the customers followed Mom. You could tell she was kind of a role model for them. Finally we were back to the customer she'd been working on. "I'd like you to meet Mrs. Hyde."

Mom pulled a lever, and the chair jerked upward. Mrs.

Hyde came into view, her big face coated with pore cleanser. She was a sizable woman with hair of two colors. "We've about decided Mrs. Hyde should go back to blond," Mom said, eyeing her professionally.

Mrs. Hyde observed us through friendly pinpoints, since Mom hadn't given her eyes yet. "Well, aren't they nice-looking chilrun," Mrs. Hyde said about us. "Beth, you're lucky your kids aren't in high school yet. We'll be sick in bed if they close it down. It'll just take the heart out of the community. When I think of our chilrun having to commutate all the way over to school at Pinetree, it worries me half crazy. You know how dangerous the highways are. I got just the one daughter in high school myself. Maybe you young folks have met her. She's real popular. Tanya?"

Tanya Hyde.

Bambi gaped, and Mom smiled. She spun Mrs. Hyde in the chair, saying, "I think when we get you right back to blond, a nice feathery cut like mine would be just the thing. Also, I have an idea or two for bringing out your eyes. And it seems to me, Mrs. Hyde, if we parents of the community really got organized, we might just be able to save our high school."

"Do you really think so?" Mrs. Hyde searched the mirror for signs of improvement. "I'd sure hate to see my old high school shut down. Them were the best years of my life, believe it. And you can just imagine how important a good education is to my Tanya."

I could imagine.

Mom was operating on Mrs. Hyde at her top speed now. She replaced the pore cleanser with Rubiglo blusher and used just the right brush to create cheekbones. A line here and a stroke there, and Mrs. Hyde had eyebrows, even lashes. Her eyes began to rise out of her face. "A very subtle lipstick shade, I think," Mom said, applying it to the Hyde lips. Give Mom another week, and she'd be giving them all color readings.

She stood back and unveiled Mrs. Hyde to the waiting women. It was a quickie job, but it created a sensation. One of the Calhoun sisters dropped her *National Enquirer* and gasped.

Grandma Babcock was trying to stand between her customer and the new Mrs. Hyde. But the customer thrust Grandma aside, saying, "How come you never done me like that, Blanche?"

Mom modestly changed the subject. "Well, even an outsider like me can see that Hickory Fork would be lost without its high school."

One of the Calhoun sisters agreed. "Of course, when the mall went under, we lost our tax base. And I'm up to here with driving sixty miles to a Penney's."

Winona-Fay's mother bowed her head. "Losing the

163

school will break my little girl's heart. Winona-Fay's sensitive."

"It doesn't seem right," Mrs. Hyde said. Looking in the mirror gave her new confidence. "Seems to me like the school's big enough to survive. Seems like the town's plumb full of kids."

Mom saw us off at the door. Quietly she said, "What we have here is a PTA meeting. They just don't know it yet."

We were halfway up Bates Gulch Road when I said to Bambi and Brick, "Mom's up to something."

Bambi said, "Why do I have this feeling that we've got another pilot to do?"

Brick said, "I think that was the funniest-looking bunch of ladies I ever seen."

"Saw," we said.

"Saw."

# *Chapter Thirteen*

**B**y Wednesday night the PTA was meeting at Grandma Babcock's house. Every mother in the room had a new face and hair, and they all thought they looked like Cher. By then they'd have elected Mom to the highest office in the land. By then, too, Dad had been on the phone to Hollywood because he still had his contacts. Now he had a fresh new concept for a surefire show that would turn his career around. Since he owed everybody in L.A., they were glad to hear about this chance to get their money back. Anyway, you know Dad. He's always got one more pilot in him.

Grandma Babcock and Mrs. Hatfield were out in the kitchen, being the refreshment committee for the meeting. Bambi, Brick, and I were putting Mrs. Hatfield's cupcakes on trays. She'd baked them in three shapes: P, T, and A. Grandma wasn't calling Mom *Donna-Jo* much anymore. Now she was just calling her *her*.

"I'll say one thing for her," she said to Mrs. Hatfield.

"When it comes to makeup tips, she can turn a bunch of sow's ears into silk purses. My living room's full of them."

"That's the truth, if I ever heard it," Mrs. Hatfield said. "I wouldn't have believed she could pull in that many mothers without promising them Amway products. But great guns, Blanche, how's she going to make them admit their own children are in that Rat gang? You know yourself that parents can't let themselves know where their kids are at night. They wouldn't take the rap for it."

"Don't worry about her," Grandma said, meaning Mom. "She'll get around it somehow. She's crafty."

Mrs. Hatfield handed a pot of coffee to Bambi, saying to her, "Tell them it's decapitated."

We all went out to the living room to hear Mom and Dad explaining to the PTA about the new pilot they were going to film right here on location in Hickory Fork. Working as a family, we'd roughed out another script recycled from that last pilot we'd been filming before we had to leave L.A. But this latest production of ours was going to be a lot more major than Brick in his hump and the Willoughby family.

The main concept was about this fictional town that looked a lot like Hickory Fork and how all the generations worked together to return to community values. Kind of a fantasy.

Some of it could have been a documentary about the most recent weeks in our lives. But Dad explained it to the

PTA as a completely made-up story about this once-great little town that sort of went downhill. Gangs took over school. The mall got trashed and turned into a clubhouse.

But then things got turned around. Out at the mall the gang got scared by a public-spirited family masquerading as ghosts. There'd be a football game, too, and a big prom scene at the end. There'd be laughter. There'd be tears. There'd be a return to family values. There'd be a happy ending so we could get funding.

"It'll be on the cutting edge," Dad said, summing up, "with traditional values. I see this on the Disney Channel. I see a videocassette sale."

The PTA moms were dazzled. You don't get a Christie Brinkley and a Kevin Costner at every PTA meeting. Though the moms of some of the worst Mall Rats thought the true parts of the script sounded a little farfetched, they were a bunch of pushovers.

Bambi poured. Brick and I passed out the cupcakes. Then Mom made her pitch.

"It seems to me, ladies," she said, "that we can make a wonderful family film about Hickory Fork and at the same time save our school."

"Then it's worth any effort," Mrs. Hyde put in. "The high-school days were the best years of my—"

"Of course, we'll have to be sure that all our children are

in school and cooperating," Mom continued. "We want as many of them as possible to have on-camera experience."

The moms were with us now, a hundred percent. Dad gave them the smile that melts. Mrs. Hyde melted the most, but then she had the most to melt. After all, the one business in the world nobody can resist is show business. You could see spines stiffening all over the PTA. People who hadn't seen their kids in weeks were thinking about coming down on them like a ton of bricks.

"You can count on Tanya," Mrs. Hyde said firmly, biting into a frosted *P*. "And if she's there, her little friends will be too."

"Naturally," Mom said, "they can't all be star parts."

"Tanya won't have any problem with that," Mrs. Hyde said. "She's a real little team player and generous. And popular. And I've always said she had acting ability."

"So does Winona-Fay," Winona-Fay's mother said, "heaven knows."

"I'm not so sure about our Jeeter," said one of the Calhoun sisters. "He's shy."

Word of the film project had reached Hollywood before the Mall Rats got wind of it. But after the PTA meeting they knew and came roaring into school, mad as hornets that the parents had heard something before they had.

By now it was a whole different school. Dad had assigned all the faculty jobs. Miss Poole was wardrobe mistress. Coach Wire was assistant producer, and show business went straight to his head. He had a body mike and a hand-held loudspeaker and was always yelling "Quiet on the set," even when nobody was around. An early trickle of press people were here from out of town, nosing around school and trying to get the jump on each other.

There were grade-school people on the high-school side. There were high-school people on the grade-school side. Rest rooms were dressing rooms, with makeup. Bowheads and dweebs were lining up for casting calls. Bambi and Brick and I were all over, being gofers. The place was chaos, but creative.

When the Rats dropped down off Jeeter's truck and barged into the gym, they were in full costume, if you happened to be casting gang members. But show business doesn't necessarily work that way.

"Hold it right thur!" Tanya barked when she saw a bow-head with a little black leather ribbon in her hair, auditioning for the part of gang leader (female). In a sweet little voice the bowhead was reading from a working script:

> "Tell it like it is, tell it like it wuz,
> We trash everything just becuz."

A long line of bowheads snaked across the gym floor, waiting to read for the part. Tanya, who doesn't stand in lines, muscled her way to the front where Dad was casting.

Gang members never look adults in the eye. But Tanya gave the look that kills to the bowhead trying out for a part that was Tanya's in every sense of the word. The bowhead happened to be a girl named Cinnamon Pettigrew. Tanya grabbed her by the upper arm. But as I say, the atmosphere around school was different today. Cinnamon was so into her part that she thought Tanya was auditioning with her in a two-shot. She went on reading and put a little more heart into it:

> "Who we are?
> Listen and we'll tell.
> We're the Mall Rats straight from—"

"Giddoutta here," Tanya snapped, giving her a shake. It was dawning on Cinnamon that maybe things weren't so changed after all, and this was reality.

Meanwhile, Dad was getting his first look at Tanya, up close and full figure. With her matted hair and bootheels she stood nearly six feet. Her black lips picked up her Leatherette-on-Leatherette look. Feeling Dad's eyes on her, she froze, and Cinnamon hung from one of her clenched fists.

Since I was right there, taking names, I could see Tanya from Dad's professional point of view. Real life hardly ever works in show business. Tanya had overdone it. We don't wear that much makeup on camera. And her regular costume made her look like a *Terminator 2* clone. Besides, Tanya in our script had to be this basically nice girl just pretending to be bad. In the big prom scene at the end she has to be nice again. In short, Tanya wasn't right for the part of Tanya.

Dad gave her that long, up-and-down look that Bambi inherited from him. Then he said, "Don't call us. We'll call you."

In another week we'd finished casting. Because of Justin's family's social standing back in L.A., he didn't try out for anything, though he'd have been perfect in the part of Justin. A ninth-grade stamp collector got it.

Cinnamon got the part of Tanya, and Tanya wouldn't try out for anything else. Dad cast the rest of the Rattettes as Rattettes, including Winona-Fay. They were small parts, but then that's all they'd ever played. With dreams of stardom in their eyes Tanya's homewomen walked away from her without a backward look. Dad had completely eroded her power base in a single casting call.

Little Jeeter Grubb didn't play himself either. In the

script Jeeter is a good boy gone wrong and then redeemed by clean quarterbacking and the love of a nice girl (Cinnamon). If you ask me, the script was practically science fiction by this point. But Dad said it read well, and we could go to the bank with it.

You have to keep things simple for TV, so the script didn't include anything as confusing to the viewer as an eighth-grader defeating his own high school's team in the game of the season. And so Little Bob Wire couldn't play himself. He was cast as the script Jeeter because Little Bob plays better football and is better-looking. Anyway, Jeet didn't try out. He's shy.

Dad had cast the Mall Rats as the team/gang, and they turned out to be worse little starlets than Tanya's Rattettes. They walked away from Jeeter. Dad strikes again.

During the next weeks Jeeter showed up around school occasionally. You'd see the dull sheen of his shaved head in the distance. Though we had class once in a while between rehearsals, Jeet only dropped by to run the track by himself. Tanya wouldn't darken the door of a school she couldn't control. Sometimes you'd see her out in the parking lot in the cab of Jeet's truck, sulking and waiting for him to finish running.

The quality of life around school continued to improve. Running it like the assistant producer of a major film studio strengthened Coach Wire's leadership skills. Even Miss

Poole shaped up a little. Bambi, Brick, and I were repeating our roles in the Willoughby family scene. But the rest of the grade-school kids were mainly dress extras and walk-ons.

Still, one afternoon Mom came to school to give us all professional makeup tips. She made it a lesson, using Miss Poole as a model. Which was killing two birds with one stone. Miss Poole blossomed: new eyebrows, cheekbones, the works. She was round-shouldered from carrying all those workbooks around, but Mom helped her with her posture. Miss Poole couldn't wait for school to be over to show her face to the coach. Privately, I asked Mom what plans she had for Brick's teacher, Ms. Stottlemeyer. But Mom said she did makeup, not miracles.

By then you wouldn't have recognized Hickory Fork. The intersection down by Kut-n-Kurl and Bubba's gas-and-oil looked like Hollywood and Vine. Half of L.A. seemed to be milling around down there. They had to put in Porta-Johns and fax machines for the media. There was talk about installing sidewalks so they could put stars in them. Mrs. Hatfield was renting out rooms to the camera crew and running a deli from her front porch. *Entertainment Tonight* was doing sound bites. Union labor was shooting background all over town.

We don't shoot in sequence, of course. We waited for a perfect blue-and-gold afternoon to film the football scenes. The Pinetree Trace Panthers came over to play a good, clean game with the Hedgehogs, our side winning. Dad coached.

We used Angel Bottoms's Pantherettes, in different costumes, as the cheerleaders for both teams because Angel's girls had a more wholesome look. Then at halftime the Hedgehog mascot came out on the field in a repaired hedgehog suit. When he took his head off, it wasn't Justin. It was the original Hedgehog mascot from years back. Mr. Jeeter Grubb, Sr.

The camera crews were everywhere. Lighting cables wound all around Hickory Fork and across the blacktop out at the mall. The crews were astounded by the place. They were used to Beverly Center and Century City mall, and here was this ancient ruin out on bald prairie, like something left over from *Robocop*. They did a lot of mood shots of the Christmas tree, and painted the black neon blacker to film right.

We had to close the set for both of the big mall scenes, Justin's trial and the Willoughbys' revenge. By then half of the state was milling around the mall parking lot, tripping over power cables and volunteering as extras.

The big finish was a high-school prom, even though Hickory Fork hasn't had a prom since before the Carter administration.

This was a production number that took up the entire gym. We got a little arty with it. It would begin as a regular prom scene with New-Kids-on-the-Block–type music and a cast of bowheads, dweebs, and former Rats and Rattettes, plus Little Bob Wire, all of them in white dinner jackets and prom dresses from wardrobe.

But at a certain point the music and lighting would soften, and the promgoers from olden times, played by parents, would drift onto the floor in a return to traditional family values. Dad wanted to shoot this in a single take to keep the feeling fresh and the cost down. The whole town was there, on the floor or watching from the bleachers the way they did in the olden days.

By this point Tanya had had it up to here with sulking out in the cab of Jeeter's truck. Besides, she has no inner resources. She edged into the gym to see what was going on. I don't know if she got far enough to catch a glimpse of Winona-Fay hitting her mark out on the gym floor in a pink tulle prom dress (and tattoo) with satin pumps dyed to match.

But imagine Tanya's surprise at finding her own mother behind the bleachers, waiting to go on, and listening real hard for her cue. Only a favored few of the parents could still get into their original prom clothes. Mrs. Hyde was vast in brand-new silver satin, with dreams in her new eyes and a script in her hand.

This sight stopped Tanya dead, and she exploded. Banging a bootheel, she barked, "Mama, how many times have I told you to keep off school property? Giddoutta here before I lose my temper!" Even the silver rats swinging from Tanya's ears looked outraged.

Still, she hadn't noticed her mother's confident new image. Mrs. Hyde expanded, and the sound of her big hand connecting with her daughter's mouth echoed through the gym to the top girders. "Shut up, Tanya," she said. "It's *showtime.*"

We did the prom in one take. As it progressed, the lighting shaded to lavender, and we shot it through smoke. As the music segued into "Moon River," the parents as past promgoers began to mingle with the younger generation. In his old blue suit with the same carnation, Dad led Mrs. Hyde onto the floor in her enormous new dress and the face Mom had given her. They were both pretty light on their feet, swooping on the tide of Moon River. As script girl, Mom stood in the wings beside the bleachers, smiling slightly. Bambi and Justin were somewhere off-camera, too, together. She saw to that.

The whole footage ran long enough for a two-part miniseries. *Entertainment Tonight*'s Mary Hart was to report that she'd personally never seen anything that throbbed with more rough-hewn authenticity. The *L.A. Times* did a feature on us, headlined:

## HOLLYWOOD HEADS FOR THE HILLS AS NEW BABCOCK PRODUCTION INSPIRES STICKS PIX

The school was saved, of course. Hickory Fork was now the most famous high school in the state. If the board of ed people had tried shutting it down, they could have kissed their jobs good-bye.

And you know how it is at the end of a filming. Nobody wants it to be over. They even flub their lines, just to make it last, and everybody has a nice warm fuzzy glow. By the end of the prom sequence you couldn't tell show business from the truth. All the parents and the kids were there together.

Mrs. Hyde was reduced to tears of pure pleasure. By now she was so into camera angles, you'd have thought she was a big Bambi. Mom came on the set and drew her gently out of Dad's arms, saying, "You did a fine job, and you looked lovely, Mrs. Hyde."

And Mrs. Hyde said, "Oh, shoot, Beth, call me Donna-Jo. Everybody does."

And Dad turned suddenly away to say, "That's a wrap!"

# Chapter Fourteen

**W**e're back in Bel-Air now, and I'm writing this out by the pool. It's a sticky December day with a lot of brown smog and a hint of Christmas in the air. And we're back in our house on Moraga Drive. It was a question of back taxes, and Dad's on top again, thanks to the new miniseries.

Bambi, in a new thong swimsuit that she plans never to get wet, is sound asleep out in the deep end of the pool on her air mattress. She's lightly gripping a cellular phone in case Amber calls.

We retrieved our van from the steps of Pinetree High School, and it wasn't a lot more battered than before. Then we drove it as far as Flagstaff, where Dad bought a Range Rover with his new line of credit.

There's no place like home, but Dad says Hickory Fork was the best thing that ever happened to us. It really turned his career around.

The new two-part miniseries is still being edited, so you

won't have a chance to see it until the new lineup next fall. Watch for word in *TV Guide*. We're still kicking around title ideas for it. Right now we're between *Once Upon a Mall* and *Sweet Valley Keeps Its High*, so we may have some more thinking to do on that. Actually, we're probably doing more as a family together than anybody in Bel-Air—maybe in all of California.

Dad says we're going to bring everything in under budget from now on, including personal finances, which ought to keep the sheriff of L.A. County off our property. Mom says amen to that. She also says that even though Hickory Fork was only a few weeks out of our lives—not even a grading period—the experience brought me and Bambi closer together.

I guess this is possible. It didn't see Bambi through puberty, but I've noticed some improvement there. We got back to L.A. a few days before Thanksgiving. Suddenly we were back in our regular school, wearing Chanel and hitting the books, more or less. We were only there a few days before Thanksgiving, which is the start of Christmas vacation, to take full advantage of the shopping season. But Bambi and I were back at Stars of Tomorrow—same classrooms, same seats, same tanning salon, everything. It was eerie because we'd been somewhere else, and nobody else had. Everyone knew where we'd been, of course. Watching *Entertainment Tonight* is practically homework at Stars of

Tomorrow. But people are always a lot more interested in their lives than yours.

Anyway, at noon on those days, Bambi looked me up, and we did lunch together out on the lanai, like our old days in the Hickory Fork Consolidated lunchroom. The point is: Bambi doing lunch with me? Eighth grade never does lunch with sixth. Neither do sisters. But anyway we did. Mom could be right.

I've had a letter from Little Bob Wire. He says Hickory Fork will never be the same after us Babcocks. They're recycling the mall as a discount complex with shuttle buses to pull in customers from the retirement areas. And the PTA remains active. In fact, you wouldn't know the place, Little Bob reports. Since there was no point in coming to school if they weren't in charge, Tanya and Jeeter dropped out and got married.

We've heard from Grandma Babcock too. She says they're back to normal at the Kut-n-Kurl, so she only has part-time work. But she's hoping to get back into caramel corn and Milk Duds when the mall and the Mono-Plex reopen. She's planning to fly out to see us one of these days if they catch all the airport terrorists and pen them up in the same departure lounge.

Justin's definitely coming back to L.A. Bambi's counting the days and telling Amber. Apparently his mother is already back in Brentwood, trying to buy back their passive-solar Tudor. His father's planning to turn their mountaintop spread outside Hickory Fork into a conference center for the environmentally correct.

I miss Bob, and he says he misses me. He mentions that he's going to let himself graduate from eighth grade. With Jeeter off the team Bob's going to play football—for the Hedgehogs, of course. He says Stretch and Miss Poole are still sweet on each other. And I think it would be great if Little Bob could come out to L.A. for a visit. For one thing, he'd look terrific with a beach tan. For another, I won't be twelve forever.

And now I've got to wind this down. Brick has just come out of the house in full green makeup, extra eye, and his hump, as the little Willoughby boy drowned down the well. Brick's getting to the stage where if you don't keep him busy, he's a pest.

Now he's slipping into the pool at the shallow end. Now he's doing a butterfly breaststroke down the pool with his little hump showing. Now he's about to surface right beside the air mattress next to Bambi's head. And the timing's great because her phone's ringing. Bambi's just about to open her eyes, and this I've got to see.